France, Story of a Childhood

France, Story of a Childhood

Zahia Rahmani

Translated by Lara Vergnaud

Yale UNIVERSITY PRESS · NEW HAVEN AND LONDON

A MARGELLOS
WORLD REPUBLIC OF LETTERS BOOK

The Margellos World Republic of Letters is dedicated to making literary works from around the globe available in English through translation. It brings to the English-speaking world the work of leading poets, novelists, essayists, philosophers, and playwrights from Europe, Latin America, Africa, Asia, and the Middle East to stimulate international discourse and creative exchange.

Yale University Press books may be purchased in quantity for educational, business, or promotional use. For information, please e-mail sales.press@ yale.edu (U.S. office) or sales@yaleup.co.uk (U.K. office).

Set in MT Baskerville type by Tseng Information Systems, Inc.
Printed in the United States of America.

Library of Congress Control Number: 2015951743
ISBN 978-0-300-21210-5 (cloth : alk. paper)

A catalogue record for this book is available from the British Library.

This paper meets the requirements of ANSI/NISO Z39.48-1992 (Permanence of Paper).

10 9 8 7 6 5 4 3 2 1

To Lounis Aït Menguellet
and to Nicolas

Man cultivates his imagination in the place where
he is born.
When adversity and war displace him far away
he is tempted to imagine
what his life could have been without this rupture,
if only to forget for a time
what they think
of him here.

Wouldn't turning to "I"
be for him, in this case,
the only fiction possible?

Contents

Translator's Acknowledgments   ix
Translator's Introduction   xi

France, Story of a Childhood
Prologue   1
One   17
Two   45
Three   103
Four   123
Epilogue . . .   181

Translator's Acknowledgments

Thanks to Alyson Waters and Emmanuelle Ertel for their support and insight, Allison Schein and Chris Clarke for their honest feedback, and the PEN/Heim Translation Fund for its generous grant. Finally, I must thank my treasured readers: Diane, Mohamed, and Anthony.

Translator's Introduction

Lara Vergnaud

France, Story of a Childhood—the third in a loose trilogy of novels by Zahia Rahmani—is difficult to categorize. Often described as fictionalized autobiography (autofiction), the work has a poetic, nonlinear style more resonant of fiction than of nonfiction. Inspired by foreign literature, music, and art, particularly from the United States, the author-narrator employs restrained yet lyrical prose to describe her difficult childhood in an adopted country, France, all the while paying homage to her Algerian heritage. Historical events figure prominently against the cascade of childhood memories revealed by the narrator over a single day as she cares for her convalescing mother.

Rahmani was born in Algeria in 1962, amid the political instability that followed the Algerian

War of Independence from France (1954–1962). During the war thousands of Algerians—some estimate several hundreds of thousands—were recruited or coerced to fight as auxiliaries alongside the French army against their countrymen; these men were dubbed Harkis after the Arabic word *harakah,* meaning movement and, more recently, military or political unit. After the Algerian War, the word acquired a more sinister meaning—traitor. Like many Harkis, Rahmani's father was imprisoned after the war. Yet the author would later discover that her father's arrest and imprisonment stemmed from political reasons and that he had, in fact, never worn a uniform or borne arms. (This fabrication and its consequences are the subject of Rahmani's first novel, *Moze.*) In 1967 Rahmani and her family fled to France, to a small town in the rural region of Oise, a forty-five-minute train ride north of Paris. There, they would experience a new brand of contempt and ostracism. France, already overwhelmed by the unforeseen return of approximately one million repatriated Frenchmen ("pieds-noirs"), was no more accepting of the Harkis than was Algeria.

Although Rahmani sets her novel against this turbulent history, she seldom refers to the Harkis, using the term only thirteen times. During my first meeting with the author, in Paris in the summer of 2012, Rahmani, reluctant to be pigeonholed, stated that she prefers to be regarded as a French rather than a Harki or Franco-Algerian writer. Indeed, though *France* has at times been assigned to a small but growing corpus of so-called Harki literature, the author-narrator's vivid recollection of her childhood in Oise is the true force propelling the narrative. Relationships are central to the novel's emotive core. Several figures dominate: Hocine, the narrator's older brother; Madeleine, an elderly villager; Anne-Marie, a liberal teacher; and a domineering father, unnamed in an echo of his mute response to a traumatic past. And most vivid, the narrator's mother, Ourida.

In a milieu marked by ignorance and at times hostility, the reserved Ourida is determined in her efforts to ensure a future for her offspring, while keeping her adopted country at arm's length. For her children, she will "bequeath an unspoiled legacy . . . filling in a void that [they] cross with growing strength." That is her greatest gift. Through cultural education rooted in the oral tradition of Kabylie, Algeria, and transmitted through Kabyle, a Berber dialect, Ourida strives to outmaneuver what the narrator perceives as a massive machine assembling against her—the whole of France. Replete with the echoing voices of the narrator's ancestors, parents, siblings, friends, neighbors, and teachers, *France* evokes the potency of oft-dismissed oral cultures. The result: a patchwork of legends, memories, literary quotations, and songs.

But a fine thread holds this patchwork narrative together. Though skipping across space and time, often on the same page, and even in the same paragraph, the narrator always returns to an attic room in her family home in the Oise countryside. As she keeps watch over Ourida, the attic room above—once playroom, library, lounge, and sanctuary—fills the narrator's thoughts, unleashing a torrent of childhood memories.

Anchored to this attic hideaway, the reader voyages to turn-of-the-century Kabylie, where Ourida grew up, on to Algiers in the turbulent 1980s and 1990s, and forward to the iconic Gare du Nord in modern-day Paris, where the narrator grapples with the news of her mother's illness. Then back again to Oise, the verdant, curiously flat region that stars in the narrative. Though the narrator rages against the racism she encounters in her small town, she nonetheless respects the inhabitants' savoir-faire, which, in her eyes, is as magical and transformative as the mythology of faraway Kabylie. She devotes detailed passages to the now forgotten arts of cultivating poplar trees, preserving vegetables, assembling sausage casings, and crafting hairbrushes from stiff hairs and plastic, revealing her affection for her rural neighbors.

Still, the Oise village can be both haven and trap. At times, the villagers emerge collectively to alternately welcome and reject, inform and disappoint *France*'s young narrator. Hence the tone of the narrative wavers between nostalgia and resentment ("let them keep their 'before, we all respected one another'").

Equally formative, if more abstract than Oise, is the United States. The works of several American authors, many from the 1930s and 1940s, resonate profoundly with the narrator. The circumstances of Richard Wright's *Black Boy* may be foreign, but his words illuminate the narrator's own struggles:

> I don't live in a black ghetto in Memphis where everything would be off-limits, but in a white ghetto where all individuality is refused me. The word "God" is never pronounced in my presence, but I'm reproached for my parents' religion without being told why it's not as good as any other. In the villagers' minds, I'm Muslim, which for them equates to a kind of barbarism.

Later the narrator experiments with social activism, buoyed by her readings of John Reed, Jack London, Erich Maria Remarque, and Joseph Conrad. But Wright, Hemingway, Steinbeck, and Faulkner remain the prominent ghosts in the attic room. Foreign music, theater, and art provide additional outlets, but the influence of American literature in particular permeates this largely dialogical text.

France unfolds deliberately and with restraint, evoking the plain writing of Erskine Caldwell. Like the American author, Rahmani eschews excess, what she calls *gras*, the French word for "fat": "Tonight, I lead a symphony, no omissions, no embellishments. I have few instruments." This sparseness heightens the intensity of the narrative. In one of our many email exchanges, Rahmani explained, "A feeling of proximity, a shared world, a language created for the other, the foreigner, unfolds. Anything that could obstruct [my] intentions is removed from the text."

The prologue to *France*, a series of vignettes recounted from a child's perspective, establishes the novel's austere voice, which many French reviewers have described as *épuré*, or stripped down. One example: "A man is sitting on the floor, in a corner. The room is dark. He is silent and gaunt. I am told, 'It's your father.'" The spartan language draws the reader in. *Our* father calls us a whore for daring to watch television. *Our* brother comes home in a casket. *Our* mother is dying. Rahmani is also frugal in describing her characters' appearance or movement. The narrator kneels in a garden, kisses a boy on the lips, holds her mother's hand.

Rahmani's bare-bones style, however, does not exclude lyricism or poetry. *France* is lush with both. Like the Kabylian legends to which Rahmani pays homage, the novel begs to be read aloud. (Remember that the opening lines prepare us for "a symphony.") The author confirmed her preoccupation with the spoken voice of her work during our Paris meeting. She recounted that she read every passage in her novel six or seven times until she was satisfied "que ça sonnait bien," that it sounded right. I did the same with my translation, relishing the gentle rhythms of the text. When describing Hocine's endearing English girlfriend, Mandy, the narrator adds, "My brother marries this melody." The musicality continues throughout the novel:

> We scare one another in the dark forest, the trees picking up the echo of our voices, lighters in hand, bolting at the slightest noise, waiting for dawn, leaping roebucks, feeding ourselves with strawberries as tiny as teeth, rolling our bodies in beech leaves, smelling nature as if with a snout.

One of the most striking stylistic departures in the text comes in the form of an emotional op-ed written in 2002, on the fiftieth anniversary of the start of the Algerian War, and first published in the French journal *Drôle d'Époque*. In this essay, titled "Everything / One I Left Behind," reality dramatically reasserts itself. The author lambastes both France and Algeria for the abuses of the postcolonial era.

It is useful to recognize the sociopolitical context surrounding the writing of *France,* which was, in large part, a response to national unrest in France. In the fall of 2005, two young boys from the long marginalized Clichy-sous-Bois housing project outside of Paris were electrocuted as they fled city policemen. Their deaths prompted a wave of riots that swept the poor suburbs of France's major cities. The urban violence, which lasted nearly three weeks and primarily involved second-generation immigrants of African and North African descent, left some ten thousand cars in burned husks, hundreds of damaged buildings, and the country shaken by the upheaval of racial tensions.

The cry of protest threading through *France*— against the racial tensions at play in a contemporary "France on fire," the injustice of a fifty-year-old conflict that continues to punish its actors' children, and the burden of ignorance in a small town—is evident, though the narrator's allegiances to her native and adopted lands are mutable. However, it would be a mistake to view Rahmani's novel as predominantly political commentary or representative of Harki fiction in France.

True, the themes Rahmani explores in *France* and her other novels mirror those found in works written by other Harki children: collective silence and guilt, and the role of Harki mothers as guardians and transmitters of family history and cultural identity. And like other authors who write about the Harki experience, Rahmani uses dueling languages, specifically French and Kabyle, to convey the cultural challenge of integration. (Fortunately for the reader, Rahmani reveals the richness of the Kabyle language through her own translations.)

But, for this reader at least, the relationship between Ourida and her daughter transcends the novel's historical and political context. Some may be struck more by the author's insistent voice, railing against racism and familial reprobation, the poignancy of the narrator's struggle to find her place in between two cultures, the historical backdrop of a nuanced conflict that continues to fester, or the lyricism of the prose. Regardless, what Rahmani expressed to me is true. *France* is not a Harki story, or even a French story. It is a universal tale of oppression, pain, and rebellion. Transmission, heritage, and family. Identity and belonging. And most affecting, maternal love and the moments that precede a great loss.

Note: The reader can certainly understand and appreciate *France* without any knowledge of the Harkis. However, some historical background provides for a more in-depth understanding of the work, and was vital to my own interpretation and subsequent translation of Rahmani's novel. An excellent English-language resource on the subject is *The Harkis: The Wound That Never Heals,* by anthropologist Vincent Crapanzano. Building on extensive research and in-person interviews, Crapanzano explores the lingering psychological impact of the Algerian War on the children of the Harki. To illustrate this, Crapanzano often draws from the small field of Harki literature, citing, for example, Rahmani's writing as a compelling example of the "ambivalence that the [Harki] children feel toward their fathers."

France, Story of a Childhood

Prologue

Tonight, I lead a symphony, no omissions, no embellishments. I have few instruments. Percussions and flutes. Standing, I conduct a breath.

In the back, a voice calls me, "Mademoiselle, mademoiselle?"

Like the dry crackling of a tree leaf clenched in one's hand, I hear, "The jury wants a little serenade, not this score."

With my back turned, I nod. I start over. There are few instruments. Nothing omitted, nothing embellished. I remove the breath. A beat.

They interrupt me.

"This is impossible. Without a piano, without a violin, you can't. It can't be done! Play us something else. You must have a short movement, a memory, a landscape?"

I lower my head.

I open my hand. The leaf unfolds. I look at it. I see nothing but broken paths. I let it slip away. I leave the stage.

* * *

It's dawn. I get up.

For days my mother has been sick. Her heart.
I return to her bed.

This morning, I lie down beside her.

"My daughter."

And she closes her eyes.

My head against her shoulder, my hand holding hers, I curl up, I'm frightened. Suddenly, I'm tearing down walls. I fall into childhood.

I run up to an iron door. I enter. It shuts behind me. I'm out of breath. Someone tells me I deserve this, it serves me right. This happens in Algeria, I'm maybe four years old. Outside, children bang and throw rocks. I tell them, "My father will come back, he'll come back and beat you all." My left eye is bleeding.

We are woken up. It's the Red Cross. Quickly, my mother grabs us. We drive to Algiers.

A man is sitting on the floor, in a corner. The room is dark. He is silent and gaunt. I am told, "It's your father."

*　*　*

I don't move. Men in suits come and go. We are many. More and more. Everyone waits.

One night I am put in a truck. In the morning I gaze at the ocean from the deck of a boat. That night I leave the port in a truck. I walk and sleep in a hangar. The next day I leave again. We drive. The vehicle stops. A soldier lifts the tarp, the sky is blue, the sun warms us, nature is beautiful. It's wonderful.

There are plenty of children, plenty of people around us. My father talks to many of them. I climb into the back of a Renault Dauphine. We leave the camp at Saint-Maurice-l'Ardoise.

I'm sitting on the lawn of the building where we live in the Oise region. I'm little. All the children are laughing. Making fun of me. It takes me a while to understand. I'm not wearing underwear.

*   *   *

I'm holding my schoolteacher's hand. I always hold her hand.

I open the window, the shutters, and I climb over the sill. We live on the ground floor. My father doesn't want us to go out. He took the key.

I go to the super. I ask him to open our door. He refuses, he fears my father.

I insist. "Tell him that he doesn't have the right to lock us up. Tell him that it's not allowed."

He gives me the spare key.

I go see Isabelle. I show her the black patent leather shoes and the navy blue velvet dress with its bow tie of sky-colored ribbon that she gave me. I'm very pretty. It's the first time. I hug her with all my might.

I'm coloring in a children's book. I use lots of brown. I'm in the basement of a church. There's a light on. It's Thursday afternoon. The nuns are very kind. Sometimes they leave me by myself. I want to learn how to pray. They don't want me to. I know he's called Jesus.

A lady comes looking for me at school. She's ugly. She scares me. She's a witch. I run away until nightfall. I can't go back home. I'll be beaten. I make myself a bed in the cellar.

I'm at the seaside. It's cold. My father is sitting in his swimsuit. He's kept his shirt on. My mother is dressed. She takes a hard-boiled egg from her bag and gives it to him. I asked for ice cream. My father's legs are very white. I wait.

I go to cross the street, there's a loud noise, I find myself on the ground under an engine. I'm no longer moving. I hear people. They arrive, they come closer. Someone is talking to me. A fireman carries me. They bring me into a house. I pee, then someone gives me a cookie. "I saw the bus hit the eighteen-wheeler," says one man, "and then the thing spun out straight at the little girl." They're looking at me. I still wonder how I made it.

I'm singing with Frédéric. We make it into a contest of French songs. We imitate pop duos Stone and Charden, Sheila and Ringo. We sing holding hands, *L'avventura c'est la vie que je mène avec toi* and *Laisse les gondoles à Venise*. The tar that separates the lawns is a river. All the children in the building are here and we're very happy. I like Frédéric.

We break the windowpanes of the tennis clubhouse. We steal all the racquets and balls. We hate everyone who plays this sport.

I run to Madame Film's house to watch television. They walked on the moon.

I climb trees and I say, "My name is Pippi Longstocking."

*   *   *

Monsieur Tanguy's son can't speak anymore. He watches us from the window. His neck is as fat as his bulldog's. He swallowed a wasp.

I get home from school and give a piece of paper to my mother. My big brother gets home from work. My mother hands him the paper. He reads it, takes the scissors, and cuts off my two braids. I don't go to school anymore. I hide in the basement. I cry about my hair. I'm afraid they'll say I have lice.

It's eight o'clock, we're sitting at the dinner table. It's time for the TV news broadcast. Only my father is allowed to watch. We're eating lentils. My brother tries his luck, he glances at the screen. My father takes his plate away. "Don't move again," he says. At the end of the meal, he closes the TV cabinet with a key. "You want to watch television? Well then watch it." My brother is punished. He remains alone in the dining room.

*   *   *

The police are at school. They tell us to give back all the presents that Philippe gave us. We return the notebooks and pens. It's too late for the candy. We ate it. Philippe stole the money from the cash drawer of the bus his father drives.

A large box comes into our house. My mother screams, she screams while clinging to the door. I rise on the tips of my toes to look inside. It's my oldest brother with bandages around his head. People are arriving at the house. More and more arrive. I cling to the wood, I press myself against it, and look at my dead brother.

I'm standing in a bus, it's night, my dead brother is holding my hand. He's bringing me to see my other big brother at practice. I love him, I've always loved him. He's my father, my only one. He squeezes my hand.

My father is yelling at my mother. He forbids her to speak to Madame Larbi, who came to see her. She's an immigrant. An Arab woman, thin and dark, very gentle.

My mother is sick. Everyone says she's going to die. There are lots of people around her bed and I ask her, "Where's my sponsorship card, where's my sponsorship card?" I climb on the bed and I yell at her in French, "Where's my sponsorship card, where's my card? . . ." They take me out of the room.

My brother broke the large glass window-pane of the building door. My father hits him and locks him in the storage closet. He says he's a delinquent and that because of him we're going to leave. Behind the door, my brother's crying, our mother's talking to him.

Tomorrow is Christmas. I place a branch next to my bed. Maman gives me what I need to buy some ornaments. I run. I buy three of them. I decorate my Christmas tree. My father enters my room. He crushes the tree with his foot. I cry. He insults me.

I won the big marble competition. I aimed from sixty feet and the shooter went into the hole. I don't know how I did it, but it happened. I won. I know I'm not the best, but I am the champion. I accept that.

Ghislaine, Michelle, and I are making dresses for our dolls. We've settled in on the top stairs of the building. I cut out a piece of fabric, I sew a skirt for Ghislaine's doll. We're happy.

Everything is over. The apartment is empty. I'm hiding. They're calling me, they're looking for me. All the residents come down. They find me. I struggle, I say that I don't want to leave. I don't want to leave. The children are crying. We're crying. I take Isabelle's hand, I run off. My father catches up to me. I yell, "Isabelle, Isabelle!" She's my friend, I love them all.

"Isabelle, I don't want to leave!" They push me into the car. I call to her over and over. We leave town for good.

I get up from my mother's bed, the nurse has just arrived. She gives my mother a shot and leaves. I prepare her tea, I lightly butter her toast. I take her to the bathroom, I hold her, she washes herself. In the living room, she says her prayers. Seated, for a long time, pressed against the radiator. Standing back, I listen to her. From her lips only love. With one movement, she signals to me that she's done. I help her walk to the table, she eats and takes her medicine. She lies down again. On the couch, I cover her, holding her tightly in my arms. I don't want to lose her. I can't.

One

I've just made a few francs. My first wages. I'm barely thirteen years old, I buy a book. From upstairs, in the small room in the attic, I can hear your footsteps. For the past few minutes, inside the house, you've been trying to find me.

Now you're standing in front of me. I'm holding the book. A hardcover. A volume from the collection *All Painted Works*. I can sense your mood. Calmly you're trying to find me.

I don't see art anywhere but on the lids of candy boxes. What a truly beautiful thing. In 1973, we bring a picture with us from our apartment to the house in the Oise. A move of ten miles to a small village and we sink into the solitude of a century being lived without us. At this time, on our bedroom wall, above the fireplace, a young girl surrounded by flowers turns her warm and radiant face toward my sister and me. That's how Auguste Renoir painted love. Love for his daughter. Beautiful, happy, with wavy hair, she breathes a tenderness toward him that our father's gaze on us cannot arouse.

You smile, as if relieved to have found me, and ask me not to spend so much time alone. Your brother used to love reading and would isolate himself in this way. Legend has it he died without a sound, a book in his hand. Do you fear such a fate for your daughter?

"I'm reading a book."

I say this sentence to you in your language. As for the word "painting," your culture doesn't know it. I say in Berber, *"Arghigh thakthab fla painting."*

You come closer to me and I show you some of the pictures.

"Helghenth," you say.

You don't see that they're one person. All sick, you tell me. Yet it's the same face painted in each portrait. Jeanne Hébuterne, the painter's lover. You find her pale. When her beloved died, she killed herself. Jumped out the window, a

child in her belly. On the Rue Amyot, according
to the book.

"*Themuth.*"

She's dead. Again in your language.

I show you another woman. The only foreign
face. A brunette in a black hat. *The Jewess.*

You tell me her face is soaked with soot.

"*Akathoumiss eoudheegh.*"

Which also means a hard surface marked by
time.

From the shadows, thick layers of paint unearth barely parted red lips, skin covered by a
gray dust, mysterious eyes drawn in charcoal,
and brown hair under a black hat meant for the
outdoors. She's not a passerby, she's posing in
an empty space. To provoke you, I say, "*Thskar.*"

She's drunk. Hearing this word, you tell me
it's not good for me to look at such women.

"*Nequente bnadem.*"

They destroy people. They discourage them,
you tell me before retreating.

Your distrust of things foreign to your culture
influences me less and less. All your warnings,

your taboos, are unwanted. I can't want them.
I'm looking precisely for the things denied me.
I look in every corner. And it's by accident that
you lead me down that first path toward freedom.

I love Jeanne Hébuterne's face—her sky-
blue gaze, her sadness, the vestige of self-
preservation—for what remains on the surface, a
world extinguished despite its light. Whether or
not the editor consciously selected these paintings, aware of the painter's consistent choice of
model, Jeanne Hébuterne reminds me of the foreigner's face. The Jewess. And if these portraits
impose a semblance of life on the painter's lover,
it's because her own has vanished. She committed suicide.

By this time I understand the resonance of
the word "Jew." I grasp it on my own. The moment I learn what took place in Europe marks
my first disillusionment.

Paintings, pictures, images—words I can't
translate for you and whose varied significa-

tions your language ignores—preoccupy my life. You're worried. You warn me about them. But your fears arouse an obsessive curiosity within me whose provenance and motives elude you. For an image, I will defy my father. I want, as he does, to watch television. One day, I want more than just the TV news broadcast finally permitted. To witness in his presence the stream of advertisements and, why not, a nightly television show. Once the news is over, I take my sister's hand, I hold her back, we stay. What is bound to happen, happens. The naked woman. The Cadum soap one. The Dove of the era. We can only see her stomach, water dripping, soap bubbles forming, maybe a breast, she's holding a child, also naked. I feel flushed, I'm still holding my sister's hand, I don't move. My stunned father stares at me. I walk into the storm. I don't yield, I don't lower my eyes.

"Afriyi ssiagui. Afriyi ssiagui, athakahbith."

Get out of here. Get out of here, you're nothing but a whore, he says.

I refuse. *"Effagh, fagh!"* Get out, out! I tense

up, I say nothing, I remain silent, I muster my courage, I keep my eyes on the screen. And you, Maman, you're in shock. Your daughter has just tarnished a man's honor.

"*Del felam.*"

Shame on you, you say.

I understand from your words that you reproach me for revealing myself, for expressing a desire. I don't feel like I've exposed myself and I tell you, "I'm staying! I'm staying in this room just like him!"

I'm barely thirteen and I tell you, so he can hear, that the one who's embarrassed should go. "He should go, he should leave the room!" I hold my sister's hand with all my might and I ask her to not give in, to hold on, to stay seated like me, an affront that paralyzes her. She's twenty years old. Forgotten. A time bomb. A child of war, anxious and fearful, suffocated by her own desires. She flaunts her good behavior, a symptom of her denial, and unleashes vengeful barbs at me, the one who insists she be more than brave. Her words will shatter me on countless occasions, but this time I shake her resolve. She freezes. My father is powerless. He leaves the living room.

I am a girl, I have two obedient sisters, six brothers, and a father who blames me for being born. Nineteen sixty-two, in Algeria. He stayed, he says, for me. It's only when he escaped from prison to come to France that I would meet him, in 1967.

A depraved world, he says. And yet he carried me into the thick of it.

"You brought me to this country. Here I am, and here I'll stay!"

It's my first victory. I'm proud of it, very proud. I've always watched television in secret. I want him to know. As for the world? This televised storyteller is how I learn about it.

"Nothing in this country should be forbidden me. If we're here, it's your fault."

* * *

At this moment I want to cloak my father in shame. I've just won a battle. And I spend the whole night in front of the TV screen, alone, thinking about my victories to come. But which ones? I've suddenly entered the world of adults. My father has labeled me definitively. "You're nothing but a whore," he tells me with his eyes. Males humiliate us to vanquish us. A cowardly, immoral act that kills the child within. It's through this death that they make women out of us. Impure bodies that need to be purged of their filth by consent or by force. Starting in childhood, our bodies, which haven't done anything and are guilty of nothing, have to be disciplined, confined by the prudish values indissociable from our gender. We are forced to reject things we can't even imagine. Evil demons who feed on pure minds, so powerful that we have to constantly watch for their insidious presence amid the colorful backdrop of our human community, learning to see the intrinsic perversion in a look, a smile, an article of clothing, makeup,

a hairstyle, a book, a movie, a crowd, a classroom, a landscape, to hear it in a lyric, a sound,
a song, a score, and to feel it in all the objects
we touch. I have to walk, eat, drink, dress, listen, touch, watch, speak, gripped by this fear.
A paranoia that sees evil everywhere. Before, I
could ignore this alienation. But now all the girls
in my class are starting down the path to independence. Mine was just cut short. For me, this
is the gravest of insults. I am not a girl. I have
become a woman. I will accept this, but on my
terms. It is only much later that I will understand the strength and violence of my actions. I
disappear. I become a ghost.

Maman, you still believe. You hope I will accept this life that has been chosen for me. But I
refuse to give in. I reject the rules you want your
children to respect. There is no letup, you, my
father, everyone wears me out. It's agony. First
I shut out your words and suspicions. Then the
strain drives me to challenge obligation with violence. I'm in constant pain, it erupts at the slight-

est touch, submerging me. I scream angrily at all of you. Expulsing my manic thoughts, I slam my head against the mirror, glimpsing the damage inflicted by my father. I condemn myself. You become frightened. You tell me that while the upheavals of recent history are partly at fault, the ones your ancestors recounted to you weren't any gentler.

Yet my own upheavals, here in this village, don't look like anyone else's. You use kindness to banish them. Fearful of losing me, you want to be by my side in spite of everything. Sympathetic, you tell me about your life as if confiding in an ally. I hear it all, your childhood, your father's love, your children, your sorrows, and your hopes. You make yourself my friend. You love me. You need to see me live. I listen to you. I say nothing. You tell me my death will be the end of you. I don't know why, but I can't admit defeat. I want to convince you that I'm right no matter the cost, and no longer have to beg. For that I will wear you out. I will go so far as to sleep outside, in the cold, under your window, in order to hear your maternal sobs beseeching me to come in. I refuse, letting myself grow colder, unaware of the limits of my extreme need for freedom. I demand that you make my father give me a key.

You came and got me a dozen times. I refuse to let it end.

You begin with your family stories. Pleasant and beautiful, they transport me. Sometimes too far. When they beggar belief, I sigh and interrupt you. I ask who is the son, grandson, grandfather, mother, daughter, or great-great-grandchild of whom? Countless times, impatient, unable to bear your legends any longer, I implore you, "Please, stop. All this means nothing to me, I can't take it anymore. I don't care about these people, I don't know them." But you keep trying. Using fables to charm me, you tell me these harmless characters, even dead and distant, will not fade away. I can't deny our lineage, you say. I need to understand it, this knowledge will help me. I care little about the truth behind your stories but I want to understand your stubbornness in telling me them. I won't know until later that by showing me my origins, and leading me on this quest, you are prolonging my life.

*   *   *

In France, we emerged from a void, a provenance without ancestors, and this denial was the price of our admission. Out there I have no past. No history. No family. My father and mother don't matter. They aren't good for anything. They're alive, breathing, but without value. Their presence is calculated only in terms of the cost for society. "They weren't raised right!" As a child, this is inflicted on me, and I swallow it whole. "Shame on them. They have nothing to pass down. They haven't left their mark anywhere. They've never done anything good. Shame on them, the clumsy, stammering fools." I live surrounded by this. There's no one who tells me, "I love you, I know who you are." I'm barely even allowed on the sidewalks. They have their dogs stand guard. Fifty meters along the path to school, all the children from one family mock my fear of their leashed German shepherd. "Bite her, bite her." One time they let him go. He sinks his teeth into my knee. They hide so they can listen to me scream.

*   *   *

Nothing but silence. I'm an outcast. I live in rural France, where they're encountering foreigners for the first time. It's a first at my school as well. I really don't want to go. Not even via a different path. Too many pebbles in my face. Thrown by some girls. The teacher asks to see me. He comes to our home and tells me, "I'm sorry . . . sorry for what they did to you." He looks through my notebooks and says, "Good work, very good, you're ahead of us. This is where I am."

I go to school. The teacher has me sit in the front row. He says to the class, "Here's a new friend for you all. She's from the city. We're going to see if you're smarter than she is." He knows I'm the best. I'm touched. I like and respect him.

In junior high I'm reunited with my brother. He's in ninth grade. This is when it starts again. I don't belong here. I have to be careful because I can easily slip through the cracks. They hit me.

It's normal with children, but they add that I
should leave. My hair, my eyes, maybe. I don't
know. On the playground, I cling to my older
brother. I look back, but there's nothing good
to hold on to. Only faces turning away. What
they want is for me not to speak to them. Afraid
I might contaminate them, in case they start to
like me. No one comes over to my house. Later,
my classmates' parents will tell me, "In the be-
ginning—1973, 1974, 1975, etc.—we thought you
ate lions. Crocodiles and giraffes even." What's
to the townspeople's credit is that they told me.
They will add, "We were afraid you were going
to steal from us." Then, "Afraid for our chickens." And, "Afraid of your crimes . . ." Suspected
of everything. And for everything. No one ever
says "the Algerian War." I don't know anything
about it, nothing, and yet we're here and we're
frightening . . . And throughout this time, not an
ally in sight. Not one.

I hear, "Let them go back to where they came
from."

I understand, "Reject them and you're with us!"

It's a dead end, my parents don't have a country to go back to. Dripping contempt, people repeat, "We don't want them. There are too many!" Too many what? Me? You? Arabs? What does it mean? The language, the people, the country? I don't know. Back there? Ahead, behind, nothing but black holes.

"Their parents weren't raised right!"
Your kid returns from school and her home is a void. I drop off my things. I take off. Everything I don't understand is catching up with me. I see my parents, and I run away from them. I tell myself I am not theirs, I need to find out who I am. For that, I have to be free. I tear myself away, I erase all trace of them. What's more, I want them to suffer the same pain that's destroying my life. Faced with such betrayal, people give up. But my parents become impassive, they wait. Reminding me of the parable about

the vein of marble, which, sandwiched between two layers, can be extracted only by the sweat of man.

My mother refuses to back down a single inch. She doesn't want to fail.

"You deny me, you ignore me? Well, while I wait I'll talk to the birds . . ."

It's important to recognize the harm being done to the child through mere words. The insult to his or her way of life delivered in good conscience. "They're marginalized . . . We're concerned about them . . . Their religion can't . . . They are . . . The thing is, the poverty in which they . . . We can't accommodate them . . ." And as for the child, what's there to support him or her? What's he or she left with? Do the parents really have nothing? Nothing noble? Nothing the child can respect?

My mother isn't allowed the act of transmission—to pass on all that she possesses.

* * *

In France, I endure, I resist. An entire society mobilizes against me, aware of the harm being done. Crushing my future to better rejoice in my failure, it's working toward my disappearance.

Maman, it will be the fight of your life to combat the amnesia demanded of me. You understand that the renunciation of our culture will destroy me, and all your children. In adversity, one risks everything. You know this firsthand. So you outsmart negation by evoking grandeur. I hear you describe the kindness of man as a fact. And we are all a part of this miraculous world of justice and fairness that you carry with you like a storyteller unconcerned with her surroundings. According to you, men and matter can transform themselves of their own will and your internal world map ignores all frontiers.

In your language, you describe to us, through examples, a line of men and women of unparalleled feats. We need to keep them alive and un-

touched by time, you say. You like to repeat that
without them history will lead us straight to a
shipwreck.

You call this lineage clever. And I finally
understand how you're using our ancestral heritage. You present it to me like a tale from time im-
memorial that reenchants me, further sparking
my curiosity, especially about your language. To
the extent that I can't brush against a tree without thinking it might also have feelings. "Who
knows?" you say. My dawning reason coexists
with warm visions populated by vivid, unidenti-
fiable figures, whom I sometimes sense nearby,
observing me. They patiently watch over me.

In France, I can't share what you want to
teach me. I would need, as you did, to describe
the world around me without restraint. But
there's no audience before me.

"So what? You can be a storyteller in any language," you say. "I still have things to tell you
children."

*   *   *

And they are unending.

I need to understand where your language comes from. You never waver. And sometimes when it seems like I'm winning, you retreat without ever admitting defeat. You use few words in battle. *Waldin, Thajadith, Lejdud,* and *Din* are the ones that strike me the most, stumbling as they do against the reality of our lives in France. These words, independent of all religion, call out for a kinship of men and women who bear the weight of the world without ever breaking our hold on it. Enveloped by the legends of our ancestors, you say, we are living among familiar guardians. Obliterate them and we risk disappearing.

"Those who protect you. By calling on them, your actions will be noble."

"*Waldin,* those who brought you into the world."

"*Thajadith,* those from whom they came and therefore from whom we all originate."

"*Lejdud,* the guidance of those who watch over our movements."

"*Din,* action through speech."

With this last word, you remind us of dignity, honor, and give-and-take. One can't be practiced without the others. It pains you to teach us about *Din,* it reminds you of our own failings. According to you, we were born within him.

But how to transmit these words? If you had lived in your country, I don't doubt that in your community without books you would have known how to hone your weapons and perpetuate, through us, what you believed should still belong to *Din.* Speech, in all its possibilities. But in France, you're focused on combating French society and its certainties about your children.

You refuse to integrate and, fearful of a deadly contagion, you impose your rules on us. We can only speak to you in your language. You teach it to us even through our closed ears. You enthusiastically acknowledge our academic achievements but refuse to understand their meaning. To you, knowledge doesn't guarantee a future. It's up to society to assume its role.

Whereas you never abandoned your fringed scarves and colorful dresses, we aren't permitted to reveal any exoticism to the outside world. Polite, smiling, and clean. You have such an aversion to an unclean backside that you teach us the techniques for rinsing under any circumstances.

"Dishonor will not touch your bodies."

Settling disputes with the principle "without shouting, there can be no blows," you forbid us to raise our voices in your presence. You banish violence from your home in order to awaken an awareness of our humanity within us.

"You are not what they think you are."

And lastly, these guiding words to shield us from others' contemptible expectations: "Do not become what they want you to become."

"Equipped with all these rules, they will respect you," you say. "You will be judged. But never condemned."

You ignore the society that surrounds you so politely that no one can reproach you. You never go outside. If someone comes to you, you welcome him or her with grace. They always leave moved, carrying a gift you offer without a word. In this way, you make everyone who knows you come directly to you. In a country that isn't your own, you never go toward the "other." You don't want to trespass. That's how you view yourself, the foreigner. They can't, you say, ask someone to deny who she is.

You don't want to be cut in half. You wouldn't risk such an affront. You're able to fulfill that ambition all the while protecting us from your withdrawal. Rather than facing an uncertain future, we are living at this time as if nailed to the mast of a ship during a storm.

*   *   *

Against all expectation you refuse to assimilate. You say you love this country that permits this. Here you are nothing but a silent storyteller who leaves no trace. A firm believer in your heritage, you bequeath an unspoiled legacy to your children, filling in a void that we cross with growing strength. Later, you will share your language and culture with your children's spouses and companions so their daughters and sons can understand that they come from a rupture you view as a blessing. You will also want to approve their names, as if to assure yourself that together they will be the custodians of a just future. Samy, Mira, Sarah, Yannis, Mouss, Hacène, Mouloud, Kennan, Nout, Hayet, Idriss, Sabri, Taina, Tissem, Esteban, and Inès embody that wish. Let's hope they don't think of leaving.

When you go, leaving me alone in front of *The Jewess,* I know what I have to do with this image. Just like the painting, the surface on which she lies, this woman wanted to live. She found no

one to save her. My Jewess left this world, well
before the ashes.

"She's gone, all that she once was is gone,
leaving me alone," the piece of canvas beneath
her tells me. "What makes me worth hanging
on a wall now? I lied to people. Cover me with
gray . . ."

And into my body, she enters.

Two

You came into the world one spring. In 1930, when the West's gold had turned to paper, you arrived outside of Europe. And though that continent's claws were digging in deeper and deeper, your Kabylie mountains loomed like ramparts. Blessed with the power of inertia, they forced back a thousand and one incursions. Your father chose a name for you. Ourida, Woman of the Rose. He had five daughters, and on each he bestowed a carefully thought-out name. He owned his land in Tigzirt. Fifteen hectares facing the sea that, you would tell me, he used to gaze upon while holding his daughters close. Not so long ago, you could still find all kinds of fruit and shade there. As young girls, you were able to walk from the family house to the shore without being seen by strangers. Long after his death, when you were living in France, they took his land from you. They wanted to build an Algerian Miami. A new palace for the newly rich. On the waterfront, of course. In this respect, wisdom was lacking.

They built quickly atop a buried town. Yet the history of the place warned of shaky ground. But what could five widowed daughters do before the arbitrariness of a newly elected official who expropriated their lands? A dark decade extolling God's justice inflicted this indignity on you. In short, your father died a second time. A poorer man. Five daughters whose existence must always remain shameful. They left a small plot of land to each of you and new constructions blurred the landscape of your childhood. One from before time was erased. However, the rumor goes, the cinder block towers will one day fall into the ocean. They're already sinking.

Emma Halima—your mother, my grandmother—built your family home up high, hidden under the trees. She carefully painted the interior of the stone square structure, whose ruins you would later unearth. They say that even though my grandmother was strong enough to lift three men, there was no better testament to the respect she had for nature and its creatures than in her actions. In Algeria, such was her medical knowledge that more than once she saved me as a child, to the surprise of the doctors who predicted I wouldn't make it. Your delicate demeanor and appreciation for silence comes from her. Your father had an engraved copper chest containing all his precious objects, including his books. He used to read in English, Arabic, and French. He worked little and traveled a lot, too often for his family's liking. As a child, I continually shut myself off to your past. I listened to you describe your childhood as happy, and I made myself forget it. I had inherited a revolution that brushed away family sagas. In Algeria, they destroyed a miserable past for a unification with no future. I refused to believe that before, in this country of men without rights, some had spread joy by holding on to their lore and their dignity. About this, your memory never faltered.

I should tell the story of how a saber sliced off your father's fingers . . .

* * *

According to legend, a cargo of gold from a German ship that sank during World War I washes up on your shores. Once the water is calm, men set out across miles of steep rock looking for bullion. This seductive cargo forces the French military to enlist the local caïds to use their influence against the clans and the thieves. There are certainly plenty of the latter in this impoverished region, where people robbed of their futures, and unable to flee, are starving. In springtime, the search resumes and lasts for several years until a rumor reveals that one family (whose name I omit out of respect) had made off with the treasure. The family is brought in for questioning, but refuses to return what is theirs by right. The authorities try to make them listen to reason, they talk, they negotiate, new alliances and promises to come, but nothing works. The family doesn't want to relinquish the gold to the occupiers. Among the people of Kabylie, honor is at stake. A man is as good as his word, and your uncle—a caïd perched on his sorrel, proudly wearing a burnoose embroidered with gold thread, a white turban, and black leather boots—had given his to the French. The clans challenge each other and it's war against family X. There's a sword fight on horseback in the largest square in town. In the history of Kabylie, you say, no one had ever witnessed a greater spectacle. Your uncle is killed, and your father, though he had refused to act as judge (having taken a vow of wisdom and piety), finds himself in the fight as a result. With one fell swoop his hand is cut. (You become so animated each time you describe what the warriors are wearing that for a long time I believed you had witnessed the scene firsthand.) The army steps in and arrests all the warring parties. There is a trial. Fifteen men, including seven from your family, are found guilty. Deported to Devil's Island. Your father's one of them. He will stay there only a few months. When he returns, he'll want to free his relatives and will dedicate everything he has to endless judicial proceedings. He'll rent out his lands and find employment in

France, Spain, and England. He will bring them all back. Every last one. But the interminable legal battle leaves its mark. It alienates your mother, Emma Halima, for a time. The daughter of a theologian who was the head of a very old brotherhood, she shuns conflicts between Muslims. Especially when they benefit the occupier. She leaves your father to protect her name and that of her forebears. The separation will last seven years. You've just turned three years old. For seven years, you and your family resignedly accept this temporary divorce caused by a profound disagreement among kin. I belatedly understood the strength of your bond with your father. You lived with him during those years of estrangement, reuniting with your mother only occasionally, at night and in secret, because of the code of honor giving her the right, so rarely invoked, to leave husband and children for dignity's sake.

This woman, your mother, whose very beautiful portrait you bequeathed to me, allowed herself to be photographed without a headscarf. People have written here and there that women uncovered their heads at the behest, and to fulfill the needs, of the French administration. They wanted this rumor to be true, given all that it implies about the colonial interlude and its humiliations. But you have only to see my grandmother's face to discover an entirely different story—that of a woman of astounding pride who appears exactly as she did in life. Strong-willed and happy with little. She was satisfied with reigning, even from a distance, over her hill facing the sea.

Below her shoulders, the open folds of her burnoose reveal a chest covered with metal brooches and tassels. Two braids frame her face. They are tied with thin cotton threads.

As a child, I liked to believe that in reality she was the granddaughter of a great Indian chief. A Cherokee far away from his American lands. In a fit of pique, my ancestor would have left his people in search of a Homer who could teach him the secrets of the beggars, the hungry European masses encroaching on his territory as if on promised land.

Passing the Strait of Gibraltar, and seeing in the distance some Roman vestiges dominating the port of the town of Tigzirt, he would have come closer. Seeking shelter first on an island off the coast, he saw in these people dressed in woolen blankets, in these calm and peaceful men ignorant of deep-sea fishing or slavery, a certain resemblance to his brothers. He advanced and made shore. They welcomed him, he made himself understood, and they knew that he was a good man. Then they wished him a happy union with a noble family and my grandmother, his descendant, was their worthy heir.

In France, I could have nothing but unusual and heroic ancestors. This transfer of family history through fable occurred thanks to my mother's skillfulness. All other realities were denied me. My people weren't a part of the history of man. I didn't even have a people. I came from no one. My kin never entered the human ad-

venture. They were neither discoverers nor van-
quishers and made the mistake of never putting
an end to anything. Absent from history are the
silent, the eternal dreamers struck by the war-
rior as they sleep. The dreamers, who didn't
know that such violence could befall them,
hadn't armed themselves. And I, whom they
trained with sword and spear, had to become a
conqueror or die.

The walls of this attic room host the few drawings that my brother traced in black ink during what we both called our American readings. Mounted Yankee soldiers cavort with cowboys and gallop out of a canyon, swords drawn, as if heading toward a battle taking place right in front of us. Opposite them are Indians momentarily frozen around a fire, casting shadows on their canvas tepees. The wall evokes a calm and serene feeling that makes me think my brother identified with these figures. A supplicant holding out his hands is painted in another spot, copied from a book of photographs of Chinese sculptures taken at a recently unearthed burial site. The discovery of hundreds of life-sized models, captured in the movement of a procession, shocked the world. A rich prince had wanted his subjects to accompany him. He arranged their statues in his sepulcher, giving humanity a three-dimensional snapshot of his people exactly as he wanted them, fervent and distraught over his death. The shadow of a male

Medusa appears on the last wall, straight out
of a Moebius comic strip. A woman's naked
and languid body is reclining against his head,
a metamorphosed string of algae that offered
me a glimpse of feminine confidence exposed in
all its sensuality. My father never came to this
place, yet still reproached us for spending too
much time here, escaping him. He saw this attic
room as nothing but a void whose inner workings eluded him. It's a miracle that our refuge,
which welcomed each of my siblings and me as
if into our own kingdom, has kept these traces of
our adolescence, this shadowy setting intended
as an homage to our readings.

The fictional characters who crossed the
Atlantic are many. They reduced the ocean sepa-
rating me from them to the surface area of this
narrow hideaway. Like a decompression cham-
ber, it made me forget, for a brief moment, the
tumult of my life in France.

* * *

American literature taught me, and not gently, about a people. It described them without shame, showing me their humiliations, cruelty, and debasements. These trials in adversity, which I witnessed through my books, sparked a desire in me. I wanted to learn everything about the American people and the violence that brought them into the world. If I had never discovered their tragic fate—that of their black children and of all the women and men torn from their homes, fighting among themselves—I would have made a singular, constant mess of my life.

Algeria is behind us and war has displaced my family. It's brought them to an airport tarmac, where they await the arrival of the white bird that will lead them to their chosen destination. But I see myself flying toward America to join that nation's sons whose voices have miraculously reached me. My brother is the one who buys those first American authors, on his

English teacher's advice. When I see him reading all the time, even during meals, a new curiosity awakens inside me. Can you remain silent
for so long under the mere influence of a book?
I pretend to walk around him, to take an interest in his reading, while I'm really dying to ask
what's happening to him.

It's possible that my brother's childhood experience was different from my own. He could
have lost hope, but he doesn't. Children should
like school. My brother is wild about it. Arriving in France at age eight, he slips into life like
an eel. He overcomes every obstacle. My mother
told me once that my brother, a watchful com-
panion during all my tribulations, was touched
by an angel. He'll be the first in the village to
pass the baccalaureate exam. When the results are announced, my father pulls away, instead of congratulating him. So be it, Hocine
learns his lesson. He confounds our father's expectations and develops a delicate way of deal-
ing with others. He wants to be good. He learns

everything he can. At fifteen, he teaches himself martial arts and recruits disciples. He trains with surprising willpower, sending bits of tethered wood, chopped broomsticks, and salvaged hoops into flight around his body, testing their resistance on himself. This is the era of Bruce Lee, whose karate we study through a variety of books, movies, and instruments. My brother sets out to make and showcase the latter in a confined area of the house where he receives his students. He will attend the conservative University of Assas, telling me it's in the belly of your enemy that you can gauge the strength of his ribs. For us, he is the source of serene joy. He will become the king of speed on ice skates, on roller skates, on a toboggan, on a bike, in a car, as well as a marathoner, an emcee, an English translator, a pirate radio commentator, an illustrator, and a painter. He takes an interest in the life of Emperor Haile Selassie, faithfully adhering to his philosophy all the while remaining democratic and liberal. He will become a news photographer, a jet and ultralight pilot —

frightening me every time he waves at us with a
dipped wing above the house—the director of a
haute-couture label, a music producer, a game
inventor, practicing them all ardently in order
to better understand people, he says. He studies
chemistry and fancies himself a discoverer and
a specialist in plastic waste and water filtration,
then an environmental engineer, a community
organizer, an advocate for reading to children,
and the father of a joyful family. He's scared of
nothing and blessed with a unique and striking
manner of speaking. His sense of fair play dif-
fuses all violence and fear. One day, he intro-
duces Mandy to us. His English girlfriend. So
English that she doesn't sense, not even a little,
our shock when we see her. Tall, slender, almost
ginger, with jeans molded to very thin legs and a
reed of a voice captured in a language that could
make a bird cry. We had never heard such softness. Mandy sleeps in the small room. She stays
two weeks and quickly returns. For every holiday
and then for a long time. I want her as my sister.

Her brother, a bass player in London, supplies us with vinyl records by the dozen. And our collection grows like a record dealer's. I'm twelve, she has me listen to her passion. Rock music. I don't understand English, she teaches me the words. I love the Doors. She translates "Strange Days" for me. I love and I listen. Without end, I listen. And I find my idol. Patti Smith. I want to know everything about her. I learn. I learn about this tough woman with the unusual voice. Our room becomes a music lounge where one culture sings me promises of a man torn from the rough. My brother marries this melody. Gentle, attentive, and beautiful.

The attic fills up with this culture and writers will reign here. I'm pulled in as well. I don't think I wanted to imitate anything, it's the era that found my brother and me. I don't read French literature. I'm uninterested in that history and I know nothing of the failure of its bourgeois cycle. I seek the displaced man and his hopes. I seek to understand the pathetic origins of shame and dishonor, as well as my own neighbors' cycle of poverty, their convictions, and the authority behind their certitudes and words.

I read Hemingway, Fitzgerald, Steinbeck, Caldwell, Melville, Faulkner, and Williams. "Of course all life is a process of breaking down," wrote the author of *The Crack-Up*. At this time I'm in search of a refuge, somewhere I can hide from the disgrace to which I'm doomed by a society that stigmatizes me, and a father awaiting my downfall. I meet no peers. I want a new home.

Richard Wright. That's the first book I pick. I take it. Except for *Hansel and Gretel* and a few thick encyclopedias, I've never read any books and don't know how to choose them. At school, I prove myself. My grades are as good as my brother's. I'm like him in every way. Both of us, blessed with great curiosity and a genuine facility for learning, are going to terminate the social contract that aims to make subjects out of us. We will refuse to wear the binding garments

we're offered. As early as childhood, I break
away. Such an act marks you as a traitor for life.

I see Corneille's *The Cid*, Stendhal's *The Red
and the Black*, and other books on my brother's
desk. Molière and Rabelais. *Pantagruel* has me
hearing nothing but frightening pig burps and
squeals. I don't understand exactly what I'm
running from. An edifying patrimony that I reduce to the simple view from my narrow universe. I read *Black Boy* first. Everything about
this boy resembles me. I know today that I had
a strong predisposition to seek out similarities
in American literature. But how does it arouse
such empathy in me? This literature that says,
"Here you go, this person is a stranger in his
own country." It speaks to me of the accultur-
ated white man and his religion and lies, of the
cursed Negro, his poverty, his voice, and his invisible footsteps. It speaks to me of the half-wit
and the man made dumb by alcohol, who become criminals or rapists. It speaks of the por-

nographer, the expropriator, the white woman. And none of them have a way out.

"I knew," wrote Richard Wright, "that I lived in a country in which the aspirations of black people were limited, marked-off. Yet I felt that I had to go somewhere and do something to redeem my being alive. I was building up in me a dream which the entire educational system of the South had been rigged to stifle. I was feeling the very thing that the state of Mississippi had spent millions of dollars to make sure I would never feel."

And so a descendant of slaves, a broken man, tells me to write about this life laying me low. To get away from them.

American literature tells of its own people, and in so doing offers an exceptional gift. It describes one country's violence and the nation that emerged therein, making that story the in-

delible marker of American culture. This literature brings invisible souls of all origins, whose
voices were silenced, into the pantheon of great
men. No event ever saves these protagonists. We
don't envy their lives or their ambitions, and
yet we are drawn in by the inevitability of their
fates, which mirror those of an entire category of
men whose legacies were erased. I will learn no
greater lesson. I owe this literature affection, respect, and lifelong loyalty for describing its own
people as outsiders and for its commitment to
the displaced, the uprooted man and his path.
Through translation, American literature made
its invisible souls our own. Forever linking us to
a condition shared by anonymous masses kept in
ignorance of their number.

Baby Doll by Tennessee Williams is the first
to expose me to the debauchery of desire. Because of the excitement provoked by this book,
I want to find others. Colette comes to my res-
cue for a brief moment. But with the exception

of *The Ripening Seed,* there's nothing in the descriptions of my heroine's daily life with which I can identify. I find the conventions and mores of her environment too menacing. *God's Little Acre,* and the tension and crude longings manifested within, better represents the inhabitants of my world. Those who live nearby and relentlessly force the sexual taboos of "my community" to weigh upon me. The vulgarity I discover in these authors' books can't help but remind me of my father's warning. "In this country, only prostitution awaits you!" The gravity of this threat, which preys upon me, is evident.

I can't live like a little girl fantasizing about love. I've made a leap to adulthood that leaves me few possible daydreams. I have to remove boys from my sight, ignore their existence and the adolescent ritual of seduction. It isn't until much, much later that I understand my father's words: "In this country, no one is going to make room for you."

*   *   *

Algeria, my family, slavery, the black man, the Indian, the impoverished white man—I understood conquest, contempt, domination, the marginalized man. I learned all of that. But there was something literature couldn't teach me, couldn't test me on. When I learned it, I stopped dead in my tracks. My world shifted. Auschwitz pulled the ground from beneath me when I hadn't known a thing about the genocide of the Jews. Renoir, Modigliani, Steinbeck, Faulkner, and the others were quickly put away in a drawer. The deafening roar of this information would be too much for me. The crime was overwhelming, and I would understand only much later that this impact was part of its great victory. Was it worth it to assimilate, to believe in a brotherhood to come, to proudly bear the flag of a universal culture, when the child brought to Europe must learn that its best representatives were exterminated here? In the wake of this lesson I became a timid, distrustful, and watchful adolescent, relinquishing myself only reluctantly to the culture feeding my paralysis. I would need time, lots of time and wandering, to understand that I couldn't distance myself from the European. I had to walk at his side. I was a part of this defeat, just as much as he was.

I come down to see you. On my advice, you move your arms and legs. Maman, you need to walk, you need to get some exercise. The news of your sick heart, worn out say the doctors, affects me more every day.

When they called me to say, "Come, it's our mother," I hung up and left right away to be with her. Fearful of hearing the worst, I didn't ask a single question. I walked all the way to the Gare du Nord. There, I learned that my train wasn't leaving for another two hours. I wanted to keep moving. I was afraid. I called my boyfriend. He was at work. "I'll meet you in Paris, to drive you there," he said. I didn't want to wait. I told him I was going to walk, until the last café before the highway, and that's where he would find me. Behind the station, overlooking the long corridor of train tracks, I saw the world as it was captured in a frame that didn't include me. Everything was slowly coming to life on a movie screen I couldn't see. A deep feeling of uselessness swept over me. For the first time, I felt like a photographer. I saw the world outside of me. I wasn't part of it. My mother. The thought of her death was overwhelming. I pushed it away, I became a ghost, my body disappeared.

I wrote: It was bound to happen like this one day. And we don't want it. They tell you, "Come, it's Maman, it's serious." You don't ask questions. The idea of the worst frightens you. You say, "I'm coming." You pack your things, you walk quickly to the metro, holding back your distress and your tears. They tell you, "Come." Come, because you need to be there. In the metro you understand it will never be like before. You think, if I have to I'll stay with her, I'll stop everything. Then, you want her to live, you'll stay next to her, and you say, please let her live, I want her to live, she doesn't deserve this, she still needs to live. At this instant my brother calls me. Her son, her sweet darling, who's going to be a daddy. He's crying. He's crying at the idea that she will never see his child. He's scared and keeps crying. He tells me how our mother cried out in pain before she collapsed, that she's in intensive care and that nobody will say anything. That what she has and what's hurting her is still there. There's too much of it for a heart worn out from giving so much.

I don't want to write, but doing so here outside at this café table is keeping me from losing myself, and the love is there, intact, urgently leading me to see her. I don't want to write anything that may have already happened and that I don't know about, I want her to live, to still be alive and no longer in pain. I don't want to be defeated. I want to believe in a hope, to see her alive. I'm scared of her death, and selfishly, of my own. I'll hold on, I want her to live, I'm waiting, and waiting. I want to see her, look at her, want her to live, Maman I love you so much, I've never loved like I love you, I only ever loved you more than anyone else, I love you Maman, I

don't want to write anymore, I want to see you,
I'm scared of my own death, I'm waiting, feet in
the leaves, for someone to come get me, I want
to see you, I want to take you in my arms, crawl
in your bed, tell you I love you, I love you, my
only, only love.

It's done. I recopied the passage. I took ad-
vantage of a loved one's presence here to blindly
rewrite the traces of that Thursday, October 20,
2005. Since that date, I've counted down the
days to this period of uncertain convalescence
I'm spending with you.

At the hospital, your children are crying.
Everything is collapsing for us. Without you,
how to live? This country was you alone. Without you, we aren't really here. What's going to
become of us? Where are we going to live? Can
we stay after all? Should we stay? Where could
we go? You're our homeland. The only one able
to welcome us. And if we bury you here, we can

no longer leave. What are we going to do? We
can't decide on our own. Although we thought
you might have liked to join your sisters and
parents in that square in Kabylie facing the sea,
you never wanted to talk about it. And mean-
while we're panicked at the idea of staying near
your burial place. Suddenly understanding that
if we take you back to Algeria, we won't stay,
but we'll have to go somewhere else, and never
return here. We're gripped by an irrational disgust for a France on fire, which tarnishes us to
no end. Tarnishes our children who, born here,
are constantly forced to justify themselves in a
schoolyard that perpetuates insult and abuse.
My nieces are weary of all the nastiness directed
against them, "the Arabs," "the Muslims," to the
point that they finally tell me they don't want
anything more to do with a playground that con-
fines them to the space within the Koran. They
embrace that book smiling, they say, in order to
better preach the virtues of Gandhi. Preemp-
tively shielding themselves from the violent

shock of learning that, even born in this country, of a family that believed in a future for its children, they will never have a homeland.

Today you ask me for your kohl and the olive tree wand carved for you by a small boy in Algeria. I look for a long time and you smile when I hand it to you. You moisten it to outline your eyes. I turn away, hiding my sadness from you.

"Why are you crying?"

"Because of all the pain we inflict on children," I tell you.

You smile at me.

In Algeria, you gave away my clothes.

You gave away our money.

You gave away the video camera.

You gave away the household linens.

You gave away the coffee, sugar, and sweets.

You gave away the spoons and knives.

You gave away your house.

You gave a son to your daughter.

You raised a German.

You married a widow to a widower.

You paid for gravestones.

You told your stories to poets.

You applied henna at baptisms.

You sang praises during celebrations.

You adopted a soothsayer.

You healed a mute child.

You gave a home to that alcoholic man until his death.

You sheltered the beaten child.

You gave a home to all the lost souls who knocked on your door, giving them our beds and our shoes.

You cried and prayed for a burned child so much that today he sings. Demanding your presence for all his joyful moments. Tomorrow he marries.

You saved lives over and over again, buying a workbench a cow some goats a car a machine a motor a workshop a tractor a grocery store and many other things that I don't know about so that over there, in your country, those whom you know live decently. And through these lessons in generosity, you unknowingly granted us the best cure against unhappiness.

I kiss you then I leave so you can fall asleep. I go back to my attic room.

You won't be able to surprise me here anymore as you did when I read Hocine's abandoned books all night long. You would come upstairs noiselessly and tell me, "Go to sleep."

"I'm not done."

You never insisted.

Now that your legs will no longer carry you, it calms you to know I'm up here, watching over you in your old age. As a child, I ask you to never throw away my old papers. Disregarding your fixation with newness and freshness, I make you swear you'll keep everything I want preserved. Your sons and I possess few things. But like all children we want toys. So we obtain them. And since they are rarely given to us as gifts, we use them with complete and careless abandon. Crushing and misplacing each dismantled piece in a corner of the top floor that has been transformed into an open playroom with no rules. You desperately try to clean it on count-

less occasions, regularly sweeping and emptying
the room of all that seems used and pointless
to you. You unapologetically throw away elec-
tric train tracks, Meccano parts, puzzle pieces,
miniature cars, model bits, Monopoly money,
dice, cards, tokens, cubes, Big Jim arms and legs,
and every 45 single missing a sleeve. Time and
again, you strip apart what seems like just an
old stereo system to you. You keep the speakers
and give the amp to an antiques dealer passing
through who briefly becomes one of your allies.
Your voluntary ignorance of all things techni-
cal, and of how children are raised here, quickly
calms our tantrums. We're convinced that this
ignorance will empower you to repeat your actions. In our absence, during the afternoon while
we're at school, you let the antiques dealer go
upstairs and take the object of his choice. One
day, it's the entire collection of photographs that
disappears. Portraits of soldiers that the owners
had pasted to the garret walls. You tell me, a
little embarrassed, "I burned them."

I don't believe you.

"Do you know how much those are worth? Do you know what that man is going to make? Do you know?"

You don't care. You strongly disapprove of those old images. Bodies frozen on paper that threaten to dethrone the ghost in your house. The *Assass*, as you call him in your language. A benevolent guardian who can't share his home with the dead. "And they're all dead," you say. But for me, the photos and accompanying texts are how I understand part of France's history. Most of them date from the Great War. Thinking back, I remember what people used to tell me about the former occupants of our house.

In 1973, we enter it for the first time. We go through the back, the garden. It's overrun with tall, unpleasant vegetation. We clear a path of black earth all the way to the doorstep. In the house, unoccupied for the past twenty-five years, filth reigns as much as the smell of a faded, closed-up home. With the exception of the chimneys, the mirrors, and several delicate chandeliers in the hallways, emptiness and cold have set up camp. We count five faucets, a bidet, a tub, several bathrooms, six bedrooms, two living rooms, a dining room, two kitchens, including one for the summer, two adjoining rooms, an immense garage, and two attics. On the right, next to a small, covered courtyard, is another wing, a large building that contains the vestiges of a family business lifeless for more than half a century. We walk above horse stalls, crunching on flat bones, white, polished handles by the hundreds. Dozens of ripped cartons are thrown on top of them, spilling over with cut, gathered hairs so soft and silky that we pick them up by the armful. In this region once known for manufacturing brushes, the locals were hired to manually assemble the materials. They would do this work from home. Now that activity is gone. The stiff hairs molded to plastic have outlived the animal waste. We burn what remains and bury the bones. This goes on for days. The same for the brambles that pierce our skin before we reduce them to ashes. Everything is ruin and abandon. Many of the houses in the village are empty and for sale. Today, I would never be able to buy what cost my family years of work and incredible willpower. Everything here has increased in value. After a long erosion the walls were raised again. Witnesses to a decline, we were also the involuntary actors of change. We were there. We had to be. But what happened? How did we end up living alongside people so disillusioned by the future that their hearts had nearly stopped beating?

This abandon attracted my father. He couldn't stand agitation, or what followed. After wars and prison, he no longer harbored any expectations. He refused company. It was also in this village that he would decide to put an end to his life.

The house has been unoccupied for a quarter of a century. A very sad fate looks in store for the structure, portended by the cost of repairs, but even more so by the decay overshadowing the place—all the badly kept, tangled vegetation, the skeletons of bygone activities, thrown here and there, the stockrooms in disrepair, and the

imminent collapse of the walls. It's the sole vestige of a bourgeois past that the villagers helped
construct. A long piece of heavy and powerful iron is suspended over a high exposed wall,
which is crumbling and unstable. The dilapi-
dated and rusted mechanical arm could come
loose at any moment and sweep away the con-
struction bricks with it. At its base, layers of
dried entrails cover the slabs of what was once a
workshop. This is where they stretched, rolled,
and powdered animal innards to make food casings. The local women would continue working
the precut skins at home before adding a knot of
red string on the side that they tightened with
a clamp. They brought the finished product to
a factory, which delivered them to a packaging
plant. Back then people used to say, "I make
sausage casings." That work is gone too.

It was on the eve of the Great War that the
owners became more prosperous. They added
one floor to their home and constructed two
lean-tos on the sides. We will use one as a garage

and the other as a sanctum for prayer. You can read what happened next on the backs of the photographs we found in the attic. They represent men. Enlisted boys in the trenches. The cards were addressed to the master. Feigning to have forgotten they could die at any moment, the boys sent him accounts of a joyful camaraderie that implied the war they were fighting far from home was just that. A moment of brotherhood. Warding off certain death by avoiding the future, they always ended their letters with a respectful farewell to the man who, in their absence, had still employed their mothers, wives, and sisters. *With fondest memories and my utmost respect. See you soon.* Hopeful that at their return, life would carry on like before.

No male heir took over the business. A very old lady accompanied by her daughter was the one to sign the bill of sale.

I pull my notebook of poetry from the shelf. *Ode to the farmers* is a text I wrote in red ink one February day in 1974. I read from it: *Folded in half / You will die childless.* It's been over thirty years since I used to lean out my bedroom window and watch my neighbors lead their animals. They are my first friends. Sometimes I go with them to the nightly milking. I treat these farmers to whom I'm endlessly drawn as if they were my grandparents. I beg them for the kind of knowledge my parents are unable to give me. In France, the assumption that my elders should take an interest in my schooling doesn't apply. My loved ones are confused and fearful about who I am to become. They prefer to ignore and avoid my future. I'm a threat to the cohesion of my family. So how can they help with my questions or problems at school? In reality, neither my brothers nor my sisters know. Yet they're forced to teach me, to put on a painful masquerade without complaint. Out of fear of my father, my siblings improvise their role. It's often brutal, lacking in judgment or recourse. They themselves are isolated from their peers and from a clear understanding of what they should be doing. My absences or withdrawals are momentary oversights. Until my father's invariably stinging call to order.

On the farm, I enjoy rare happiness. An elderly couple whom nobody visits, whom people find taciturn when they are actually just lonely, always welcome me without ever stopping their chores. I leave my house, I arrive at the farm, I relieve them. With my quick arms and legs, I do my work. I spread the hay, I go back, I collect the alfalfa, I distribute it. I pour some water, I sweep. At the henhouse, I crouch down, I pick up the eggs, I feed the chickens. They don't eat them. They collect them. Dwarf chickens in particular, which are the source of endless wonder for me. They come in every color. Same thing for the rabbits. Long-haired, short-haired, red, black, white, multicolored, tall, fat, small, they hop around in big families. I like to give them scraps. But I would never eat rabbit. At night, I sit at the table while the farmers do their tallies. I stay until sunset, the television on in the background. I understand that they aren't making any money. That they're working hard. That they're under contract. That the land is rented from the one big shot at the agricultural bank. When he arrives, I leave. It's a sad moment.

I don't know why, but I am somewhat reluctant to write down their name. It's the name of another time. A name that no longer exists. A French name that has disappeared. Saying it evokes an entire country. Monsieur and Madame Madou. That's what they were called. No one here remembers them anymore. They're dead. The barn smell, the animal droppings on the road, the mooing of cows going home, the children racing behind them, the wild brawls between turkey cocks and the rooster who did as he pleased, all that is gone. Now the street is smooth and runs one-way. The sidewalks decorated with flower boxes are as wide as avenues, and gas runs underground just like the electrical cables. The blissful silence came at the price of several disappearances. Rural France was finally repopulated, but its human activity can be summed up by the noise of lawnmowers. After a long period of mourning, our village prettied itself up, but rabbles of children no longer run through its streets. And the Mount, the sandy, wooded hill against which our houses lean, the spot where as a child I spent sleepless, fright-filled nights with my school friends, has become a protected natural site, one of France's historical woods. No one sleeps on the Mount anymore, and parents no longer take strolls up there. When I'm struck by the urge to take a walk, I always return to the hollow of five oaks where we used to build fires and hang hammocks between the trees. Everything is picturesque, as is fashionable. A historic site, we say, an ancient forest, we believe. And yet never has nature been more abandoned by man. Now there are educational trails marked by arrows and reserved for nature enthusiasts. This sanctuary beckons me from up high.

As children, we would run up the Mount, afternoon snack in hand. A reflex handed down through a noble tradition drove the town's inhabitants there. They would collect edible plants and firewood, cut frail, uprooted trunks, and dig up creeper plants that rarely exceeded a finger's breadth, and which seemed suited for our small mouths as we imitated smokers. In winter, when the first snowflakes had barely fallen, we climbed up with large burlap bags and treated ourselves to sled rides down to the bottom. I began to dislike roads because of the existence of this lofty, nearby wood, which is prolonged by the national forest—a regional marvel that boasts even more majestic varieties of flora. The rampart of trees enveloping me like a gentle and humble mountain brings me peace, a soothing tranquility. She represents a need. The desire for a secular, reassuring feeling. I don't like homes devoid of it. I need a landscape in order to live.

Few people pass through this place, now reduced to a cul-de-sac. There are no landscapes like it in Picardy. Typically everything is flat. And yet it's here that our parents mutually decided to settle us. My father, who distrusted his emotional attachments, wasn't interested in con-

templation. So that's not what guided his choice.
He needed a dead end. Meaning a defined life.
A bath of constant, untroubled water. For me,
that expanse is named Rue du Général-Leclerc.
After a World War II hero. I didn't know he
existed. When I discover who he is, I am overcome with pride. I live on the street of a noble
man. A liberator. I learn the names of great men
through their battles. At one end of our block
lives my friend Hervé. At the other, Martine,
Cathi, and Philippe. So there's this street, the
Mount, and the forest. Each morning, we take
the bus to the junior high. Five kilometers away.
We leave at 7:30, and at 4:15 the bus brings us
back to the same road. The school day unfolds
in the following way: Once in the schoolyard,
we talk for fifteen minutes. At 8:00 we line up in
front of the classroom, waiting for our teacher.
At 12:00 or 12:30, according to the schedule, we
have fifteen minutes to eat. Another fifteen minutes later we return to our classroom. Two ten-
minute recesses punctuate our day. At 4:15 we all
get on the bus. We say hello to our driver. Always

the same one. We play, we sing, we talk during
the ride. Once we get home, we have a snack.
At 5:00, the village street is ours. I visit lots of
houses. Those where my school friends live, the
farm, and also the homes of Mia, Henriette,
Yvonne, and Madeleine, widows or old maids
whom I love for the gentle wave they give me as
I cross the street.

I lived with them for ten years. Until I left
for Paris. They endowed me with a strong sense
of humility. All the villagers I spent time with
were workers, but none of them owned a book.
Entering their homes didn't come easily. So
why did I do it? I wanted to. I was suffocating.
I crossed their doorsteps like a kitten searching
for its mother. I entered. I didn't have a choice.
Those who now occupy these vast residential
areas, who came from the Île-de-France region
to encroach on our isolation, know nothing of
this shared past. Unlike them, strangers here, I
am an inhabitant. Family.

To the others, the old timers, my life matters. As does that of my mother, a woman they know and respect. When I come back, I'm afraid of running into them, in the street. I'm afraid of their attention and their kindness, which intimidate and move me. My rare outings in town, my marriage that isn't happening, the children I don't have, my boyfriend no one meets, my absence, I am endlessly reproached for all of it. I sense they haven't forgotten the dark past, the false starts. They are ashamed of it. They ask me to come back, to settle here forever. I have an infinite tenderness for this village and for all that it retains of our life experiences. Not so long ago, a villager teasingly reminded me of my childhood. "Do you remember?" she said. "You came to our homes and you asked us to change our ways. We were supposed to work for the good of all. You told us the baker would wake up early to make us bread and that money would disappear."

It's true. I did it with a certain fervor. I knocked on their doors and I said, "I want to talk to you." No one could have turned me away. I was a child. I wanted to convince them. At fifteen, I

advocated constant revolution to everyone. I became a Trotskyite merely by reading *Ten Days
That Shook the World* by John Reed. I was open
to any and every enthusiasm. I wanted to win
them over. I wanted them to like me. I couldn't
live anywhere else but there. With them! I had
nowhere else to go. I owe this frenzy, this rush
to live, to the breadth of freedom my mother
granted me, prompted solely by her conviction
that, even free, I wouldn't betray her. I chose
to dive in unprotected. Testing out all the ide-
ologies possible, and alone. I too, like Richard
Wright, wanted to redeem my being alive by
existing, by being included in my own country.

hy are we here?" My father doesn't answer me. This is the only question that disarms him. "Why? Why did you bring me here?" If one of my parents asks me for something, I retort with this question. "Do the dishes." "No, why am I here?" "Cook." "No, why am I here?" "Help your sister, stop behaving like that, stop reading, help, help out around the house." "Why did you bring me here?" I've always found myself on the outside.

When I'm twelve, I'm told to go home. "Go home, you're a Muslim." When I'm twelve and can't bear to be in my own house, I'm told to go. "Go home. Keep Ramadan." I leave, a backpack and Richard Wright's *Black Boy* in my pocket as my only company. Thinking myself a hobo in search of a better place. I don't know how long I'm gone. Four days, eight? I don't know anymore. Everywhere I go they tell me I have parents. Everywhere they tell me I need to go home. They tell me so from every direction. Someone calls my mother. I make it clear that at the slightest reproach I'll leave for good. I return. I win the battle. No Ramadan and the right to spend as much time as I want in my attic room. I am nonetheless forbidden from sitting at the table with the pure. The believers being my mother, father, and sister. My brothers have no religious obligations. This is when I begin my fast. I refuse to eat at night, even alone. My sister, scandalized by my stubbornness, grows outraged and turns against me. Taking issue with my mother, reproaching her for our complicity, she bangs at the doors to all my sanctuaries. She bangs loudly to make me come out. I don't believe in God. I tell her I can't. "Do what I'm doing. I don't want any part of their life. Do what I'm doing. Disobey." She doesn't stop banging. I close my eyes. I wait. I can't stand her any longer. I'm overcome by rage and anger with her constant attacks, her vulgar behavior, her taste for fighting, and her North African excesses. I grab my sister and hit her, expressing my disgust for her foolishness. She runs away, screaming that I'm crazy, that I should be committed, heaping insults on me that I reject and which her mouth alone knows how to pronounce. "*Arbi ak mweche affouwathim.*" May God eat your liver. "*Ak mi ghnek.*" May He strangle you. "*Ak mi weth sou kavach.*" May He strike you with an axe. "*Thakzent.*" Scum. I'm shaken. Shaken by these words that come to me out of the darkness. After these episodes, I bury myself in sad, desolate corners where only my mother joins me in the silence. Where did those words come from? Who taught them to her? My mother says nothing. To me, my sister is a demon. I despise this God who's given her such license. I hate and avoid her. I make no allowances. I can't understand the violence within her. I know nothing of the terrible years in Algeria or of her massacred childhood. It's only much later that I learn all that. But as a child, I can't imagine the horror she's lived through. Pushing back against the ghosts of the past assailing us without mercy, she and I compete, blindly, to shed light on their crimes. At this moment, I want the house to be everyone's prerogative and not solely that of women or girls. I want the same rights as my brothers. I won't do anything to help them. I say so, and I say so to them. Such an attitude leaves no room for compromise. As a result, I don't learn to make couscous and all the other good things that my sisters will later cook regularly for me.

Who did I get this attitude from? A teacher no doubt. A French instructor who exuded femininity like feathers drifting through the sky in complete freedom. And free she was, right up to the color of her hair and her perfume. I had never, we had never, smelled anything before her. I can't describe the shock of her arrival in my life as anything but a violent blow. A reversal of perspective. Revolution via aestheticism. She was the revolution. Beautiful, tall, vivacious, and intelligent, and the daughter of a well-known man. A first in our village.

*   *   *

She asks us to call her by her first name, Anne-Marie. September 1974. She's a highly certified teacher of literature and comes from Paris. We understand that she left for us. I am twelve years old. I inherit May '68 and the hippie movement in one stroke. Sartre, Jean-Paul. French philosopher and writer. That's her syllabus for the year. We read *The Wall* and *Nausea*. What's good about coming from nowhere is that you have nothing to lose. I do the opposite, I beat everyone. At the end of the year, I send the class average soaring.

So there was a country—ours—that produced people like her. I wanted to believe it. She spoke to us of vigilance and action, state violence and power, judgment and the freedom to critique. Because of her, we walked differently. Our bodies and gazes were transformed as a result. Reading became an exercise. We learned what emancipation was. There were no inevitabilities after all. And so I marched confidently toward my future.

But Anne-Marie will only be a mirage. What is good behavior worth when you learn, at your expense, that the exception is not the rule?

In eighth grade, my history and geography teacher violently singles me out. He refuses to let me into class. He systematically asks me to stay outside. One day my schoolmates say, "Don't stay in the hallway anymore. Come to class with us and if he makes you leave the room, we'll all go." I agree. I enter the classroom, where I'm confronted with brutal contempt. The teacher tells me, "Get out." I refuse. Blows and slaps. He pulls me by my head. Clumps of hair fall out. I cry and Hervé steps in. He's my friend. He lives in my village. The teacher hits him in the face. His eye is injured, blood lands on the walls. All the students leave outraged. I've finally won them over. We lodge a complaint. The man will be transferred. But it's already too late. Too late for me.

After all, I'm not nor ever will be a part of this

history that I'm learning. I'm made to understand that I know nothing. My people know
nothing. I have no origins. My genetic code was
cut short. And my rebellion? Nothing will come
of it.

Three

Some time ago, a man I met in a symposium told me, "You know, as children we all had the same map of France in our classrooms. And our colonies, all of them pink and far away, were the stuff our dreams were made of. I'm going to be honest with you. I'm a communist, okay, but as children we loved those territories. They were ours. Ours, you know? We weren't worried about you. We knew nothing about you. Those colonies were home to us. Ask all the men here my age, ask them, they all had the same map of France in their classrooms. And that's what France was—Indochina, Africa, all the islands. We liked it that way. We were children, you see. We loved that France. You understand. We were children and we could go to all of those places. That was our country. I didn't know a single thing about you. You understand."

"Yes, I understand. You've lost all of that," I replied.

"All of that" was a beautiful hope, a land of plenty that needed a little improvement, but whose backdrop was already in place. Some nomads, of course, but if need be only imaginary ones. "Youths, straddle our African Orient, re-energize yourselves from its light and ruins, you give new life to our art," wrote Théophile Gautier. La Varende outdid him: "Become a man—this is a land for legends." Yes, you've lost all of that, but how long do I have to keep paying for it, I thought. I entered your narrative only to get stuck in it.

"Good god, we were stupid. I mean we never even set foot there. We were so stupid. What the hell were we doing over there, huh? What the hell were we doing there? It was pink, on the map. The territories were pink and, as for us, we knew absolutely nothing about you."

"My father was a Harki," I said. "I know the story."

"We were children and they made us swallow it up, you know. We swallowed it whole. Pink territories and here we are, all in the same mess. We no longer have a country to escape to. Not a one."

He left, telling me he couldn't stand it anymore.

It was the end of the colonies too. There will be no more "elsewhere" apart from where you live. No more enemies on the other side of the ocean. It's alone that you have to come to terms with this ending—the death of your enemy.

For the fiftieth anniversary of the start of the Algerian War, a reporter based in France asks me to write an article for the Algerian newspaper *El Watan*. "Not so very long ago I would never have spoken to you," she says. "I can't talk to you Harkis."

"I'm not a Harki," I respond. "You're confusing me with my father."

Her comments are proof of a conflict that's only gotten worse. After leaving Algeria to escape bombings and the murder of civilians, this journalist now proves her loyalties to her homeland by renouncing her existence on French soil and everything it might represent to her compatriots. I write the article. I entitle it "Everything/one I left behind" and give it to my brother, my longtime protector, for his feedback.

"If they accept it," he tells me, "it will mean that the generals over there have changed a lot."

I counter his argument. "It's an article for the children," I say. "They can't refuse an article for the children."

"That's exactly why it will be refused. They're the only ones with the right to say what you experienced and who you are. And whatever you do, don't ever tell them they did the wrong thing. They're heroes, you know. Heroes."

I understand all that. But I want to believe otherwise. I submit the piece anyway. November 1, 2004, approaches and I still haven't heard back. I call and ask for the editorial desk. They tell me the journalist is in Algiers. I leave several messages, but no one calls me back. I telephone and, not knowing who is on the other end, say, "But I did write an article. The least you can do is give me a response, tell me what's wrong with it. Your newspaper requested it." They refuse to answer me. I insist, I don't give my name, I insist. And by chance, I'm connected to the journalist. "Hello, what seems to be the problem?"

"Why haven't you called me back?"

Amid a testosterone-fueled din in the editing room, she very loudly tells me, "This article is an offense and an insult to the Algerian people. It shames our martyrs."

I don't say anything. Can *El Watan* be refusing it? I'm speechless. Always the same dictum. They want me in tears in order to ease their own consciences. Later, I publish the op-ed in the French journal *Drôle d'Époque*. I read it over, now with the header: "Rejected for offense and insult to the Algerian people."

I was born in September 1962 in Grande Kabylie. I spent my first five years in Algeria withdrawn from everything and ostracized because of my father's conviction as a Harki. He was in prison during this time. In 1967, my family left definitively for France. Since then, I have made five trips to Algeria in total.

The first was in 1981. I wanted to reconnect with my parents' country and my birthplace. I cried in Kabylie. I loved the people and the land. But in Algiers, nothing of the country's recent past resonated with me. On television, I heard Arabic, a language I didn't understand, and patriotic songs glorifying martyrs who seemed to me more like ghosts than conquering heroes. The montages of images with reverential overtones struck me as a masquerade. Because of my own history perhaps, I have always had a very pronounced appreciation for the counter angle. On the television screen, I saw a people being exploited, and oriented toward single-minded worship of its own glory. As for the Algerians, they blindly followed the directive given them to love one another amid hardship. Once the emotions stirred up by the songs commemorating the dead had passed, I was gripped by a feeling of anxious skepticism. Why would anyone want to build such a nation on a single memory of a war and its violence? How would the Algerian people escape this perverted nationalism? I wanted to commiserate with their suffering. But I felt alienated by the inner workings of the political system that had emerged (seductive though it appeared) and which was forged by the idea of "Algerian-ness." Everything was exclusive. I had no place here. I couldn't say who I was without a sickening discourse about the conquerors and the conquered being thrown in my face. I was spared nothing. And so we, the children of the Harkis, couldn't return to this country. We alone elicited the violence that the Algerians, who were unable to direct it against their former oppressors, turned against themselves—here I'm voluntarily paraphrasing Franz Fanon—as well as against all the men and women who didn't fit into their leaders' plans.

Harkis were killed. Some have spoken of a massacre. But why weren't the others—the survivors who would leave well after July 5* and who were labeled as Harkis or pied noirs—eliminated? Weren't they all, to cite the revolutionary propaganda, torturers? If that was the case, were they left alive out of kindness? Knowing the emotions that the word "Harki" still triggers in Algeria, it's hard to believe that people wanted to let them live if they really were what others said—monsters. Once condemned in the public eye, how many families had their possessions stolen for the benefit of others during this civil war that is so difficult to elucidate? Those who fled the country were judged guilty of treason for life by their compatriots, without the benefit of a fair trial or even the semblance of historical research. As a result, one can imagine that

---

* On July 3, 1962, Algeria obtained its independence from France after a bloody, eight-year-long war. However, Algerians celebrate Independence Day on July 5, to coincide with the French invasion on the same day in 1830.

the Algerians, heedless of their responsibility, were able to justify the Harkis' arbitrary banishment and dispossession. We mustn't, Ben Bella* used to say, allow the model we've just fought against to survive in Algeria. But those who saw Algerian socialism at work could rest easy. That said, dispossession does not occur with impunity, and reparations are not easily made. If Algeria wants to move forward peacefully, it will need to draw on a specific type of courage to tirelessly address the current grievances against it, as well as those still to come.

In 1981, Algeria wanted to be completely monolingual. It legally imposed the Arabic language and accompanying religion on its people. Without the policy's monoreligious mandate, some segments of the country's history might have been salvaged, but neither Jews nor Arab Christians were invited to express their dissent.

The consequences of this project were disastrous. The few "French" people whom I met insisted on loudly proclaiming their "Algerian-ness," which they thought meant they were integrated for

---

*Ahmed Ben Bella was the first president of Algeria (1963–1965).

good in this country to which they had given so much. Every day they bore witness to the abandonment of Algeria's French culture in favor of a pan-Arabism that beckoned with open but necessarily empty arms. Rare were those willing to accept to what point the despair voiced by Albert Camus and Kateb Yacine was also their own. It was only in Kabylie, surrounded by my old aunts and uncles, that I found love and reassurance. They told me about their loss and pain. I was one of them, though they hadn't seen me in fifteen years. I personified the shock, still raw, that they had experienced after the Algerian people were divided. On this subject, I've said that you can't recover from a ruptured brotherhood without a certain amount of grieving. Their generosity only deepened the abyss in which I found myself. The memory of their love still haunts me. None of those family members, most of whom are dead now, ever saw my father again.

Back in France, I no longer believed in the romantic, comforting illusion of a faraway land. I gave up on the idea of ever going back. After that decision, I had to reshape my life around objectives as yet unknown to me. The process was painful. France wasn't the right place for me. In no way did this country, still overly reliant on its precepts of universalism, want to support me or be enriched by the conflict haunting me. In short, I contributed nothing. Relieved of all responsibility—and not without a good dose of amnesia—French society pretended to be unaware of my situation. According to the schoolbooks, the Algerian War never happened. And admittedly there's no trace of it in France. After all, everyone knows a silent soldier makes no noise. The war had happened elsewhere and in the meantime, I was dragging it around what seemed to be a repainted set. Behind was a layer that someone had hurriedly covered up. "Ssshhh," the French people would say. I never saw that war. Yet in my home, in our house, I saw my father's face every day. He was mute. So who could I talk to?

I grew up in a cultural and linguistic space tightly knit around Algeria. My mother spoke to me only in Kabyle. Her morals and religion came from her native country as well. The "Harki," or as we used to say Algeria-born, community that I was able to associate with in France wasn't any more emancipated from its Algerian identity than were my parents. In short, we were trapped in one moment, as if hanging in a cage swinging between

obligatory regret for life in Algeria and our hypo-
thetical entrance into French society.

I owe my break with this existence to literature.
It taught me about the black man and the pariah.
I've believed in the value of rupture ever since. I
didn't want to choose between the melancholy idea
of a lost homeland and the unavoidable abandonment of my childhood brethren. So I broke with
everything I believed was linked to such a choice.
I didn't want to be assigned to anything. I just
needed to become free. I waited ten years to go
back to Algeria. It was 1988. I went to take walks
on the mountainside. I couldn't do it. So I gave up
on vacations there as well. Then came 1989. My
cousins were happy. Everyone was starting to have
hope. Some of them began to write for the newspapers, one was going to open a cabaret, another
a tearoom. One day, one of my cousins called me.
"Come visit, I'm opening a literary café." In the
time to get excited and clear my schedule, I decided
to bring two female friends with me to Algiers and
Ghardaïa. I told them, "Algeria's changed." It was
October 1991. When the glass arrivals door opened
in front of us at the airport, we lowered our heads
quickly in the same movement of paralysis and

fear. There was an endless row of bearded men in long robes visually undressing us from head to toe. I've never wanted to get back on a plane more than on that day. We left the bottleneck trembling. "You won't go to Ghardaïa. You can't. Not three girls. Algeria has changed," said the man who came to pick us up.

Two weeks after my return, on November 11, my father committed suicide. I will never forget the few words he said before his death: "It's starting over, it's starting over." In June 1992, I was gripped by immense sadness. I couldn't stop crying over the unhappiness of my father, a man I thought I didn't love. Algeria resurfaced in a flood of tears. I decided to go back one last time. The trip was short. It took place in September. I was thirty years old. For one week I walked where a man who never spoke of himself and whose name I bore had grown up. I saw his house, his school, his land, and the hills where he used to hunt with his friends. Some were still alive and wanted to tell me about him. They did so tenderly. They spoke of his childhood and his adult life. Others who were undoubtedly hoping to reassure me told me what a good man he had been. I didn't want to hear that. They had loved him, they still loved him. As for the rest, I had my own ideas. I've never lived through a war myself. The decade that followed was agonizing for me. Algeria was knocking too hard. Each time I heard about bombings and casualties in Algiers, I would fearfully wait for a call to ease my worry. On the telephone I kept asking my cousins, "How do you do it? How do you do it? Tell me, how do you hold on the way you're holding on?"

I didn't know that I would return to Algeria one day. I came back at the invitation of a French TV station. It was March 2003. Twelve years after my last trip. I won't write here of the joy I felt during the three days I spent in Algiers in the company of exceptional men and women. For the first time I saw the face of a new Algeria. Dogmatism had well and truly given way to the demands of a citizenry strengthened by forty years of privation.

I belong to an adult, educated generation that very quickly understood that it needed to emancipate itself from any demand made in the name of community or religion. "We" are defined solely in the eyes of others. But I am the only one who knows who "I" am. It's because of our history that we, the children of Harkis, became who we are. And

whether people like it or not, we are the legitimate
heirs of a war that entitles us to tell the parties involved that we have judged them harshly. Beyond
the contempt and harsh rhetoric directed at the
Harkis by the Algerians, beyond their political
cannibalization and ignoble treatment in France,
our first responsibility was to live. Though it wasn't
painless. We had to move beyond the states of
mourning and constant supplication through which
people hoped to keep us on one side or the other.
We knew to learn from our fathers' lots in life. As
for the questions of choice, blame, and fraternal betrayal, we've lived with them since childhood. By
assuming the challenges faced by our parents, we,
more than anyone else, know what war means. The
past decade in Algeria, which saw so many men and
women killed, was for us rich in experiences and
abnegation. There are still some who would like
to believe that the Harkis live in a state of depen-
dency, be it emotional toward our country of ori-
gin or plaintive toward our adopted country. That
state is long gone. And our fathers are dead. Was
the true force of this uprooting ever duly measured?
The fact remains that our existence as "exiles" —
one that defined us and which, in my eyes, could

be a blessing if ever it was deliberately brought to light—demands an unimpeachable quest for truth. They made us, the children of Harkis, the bearers of betrayal. But to what end? All those involved should search their souls and consciences for what they hoped to perpetuate with this chapter of history. As for me, I've seen the exodus of young people from Algeria firsthand. As a result I can't help but think that thanks to the dramatic disappearance of the "other," the country has nearly finished digging its own grave. That "other" is me and all those refused the right to describe their relationship to this country in a different way.

But though that grave lies open, Algeria is still alive. May it heal its wounds and find happiness once again.

Fifty years ago, several explosions disturbed the dreamers' slumber. No one knew what the outcome of those events would be. There was a war. I was excluded from the country. I wholeheartedly hope for the Algerians that not another of their citizens finds himself in the position of having to set off a bomb in his own country. And if it happens, as it happened not so long ago, I ask that we do not condemn that man's children. Not the children. Never again.

Four

But at thirteen, I know nothing of that and keep reading. Reading all the while asking, "What am I doing here? Someone tell me what I'm doing here?" Every day, I leave my bedroom and go to one of the French villagers' homes. I do little but sleep at my own house. I have breakfast there in the morning and I eat my other meals at school. At night, I retreat to my corner. I read. I read all the time. My sister bangs on the door, she bangs nonstop. I learn the trick. I stop speaking. Except when I'm in the street, alone or with others. In houses, but not my own. I go see a friend and we make sausage casings with her mother. I go to Madeleine's home. There it's hair curlers. I open the plastic netting, slide on the spring, fold the edges, hand it to her, and she pushes in the bottlebrush. When the table starts to overflow, we make packets. Six per pouch. We staple them. "Den" is printed on the labels. The name of the nearby factory. "Take a butter cookie, sweetheart," she tells me. Outside, in her garden, I attentively follow her around. Like her, I take a hat. "Hand me the rake, sweetheart." Kneeling, I pull out the weeds. She tires quickly and sits down against a wall. I hold her hand. Tall, old, silent, and alone. I want to live with her. I lie down in her field, nose under a poppy flower. I stay under the poppy's softness, I resemble it. A fragile birth for a life too short.

Inside, we count the bags and I ask her, "What was it like here before?"

She tells me about my house, once owned by her former masters whom she watched over as a servant. She tells me, "They had horses, carts, and a car. The foreman would gather the brushes and pay the female workers. That's the way it used to be. Now I take my cartons in myself. It's impossible to get by without a car."

She has no husband and no children. She lives in her kitchen and sleeps in a very rudimentary room. The living room holds the residue of her history, invaded by furniture that belonged to the widow, the former owner. She shows me the pieces placed in storage under white sheets. I see gold decorations adorning beautiful wood. Beds, armoires, dressers. The drawers are overflowing with linens and in one spot, she's gathered together vases, pots, candle-holders, and mirrors.

"After her husband died, she left to go live with her daughter in town. The house was too big. At the end, they were using only the bed-room. The rest was closed up. It was too cold. He was a hard man. Very hard," she says. "But his wife was kind, kind and gentle."

"And the boys from the village?"

"Many of them died during the war."

"And you, Madeleine, which one did you love?"

She doesn't answer me. She often smiles at my questions, holding herself with dignity like the well-mannered young lady she still wants to be. There was only one war. The First, the sole, the exceptional, the one that killed all the town's sons. The other war, the second, was purposely shelved. Too much cowardice hidden there. The first conflict was so violent and so terrible that nobody wanted another one. During the Second, the mothers were the first to protest the conflict, allowing the Germans to carry out their occupation. The soldiers stayed for a time, in a stucco castle at the base of the Mount. We don't know if the local girls took their revenge. Who knows if there was even a single act of resistance? Contempt for Fritz in order to avenge one's only lover—if only in daydreams—killed in battle.

"Madeleine, how old were you in 1914?"

She doesn't answer me.

Her last name is scattered across the monument to the casualties of both wars.

"Madeleine, how old were you in 1914?"

Her father, her brothers, her uncles. All dead.

"Madeleine?"

"It wasn't like this before. We all respected one another."

A need for her missing masters or the desire for a past that would erase so many sacrifices made in an era when you waited for the return of the living. The boys lucky at dodging bombs, survivors of horrors, who supported with a look, a sadness, the ones to whom nobody came home. They cried alongside those resigned to accepting the death of their brothers. Madeleine, to whom nobody came home.

Before, we all respected one another.

Respect for the dead. Working far longer than the age required, your home making up for a small pension, the garden constantly cultivated until the end, let them keep their "before, we all respected one another." Heavy secrets are nestled in these people's minds. Respect for the dead and nowhere else to go. They're careful not to stoke quarrels, stifling desires beneath mumbles, they see each other every day and every day the same. They say hello, they're still there, making do, otherwise they would be too alone, walking behind the casket of the last to die, lamenting the secrets buried underground.

They tell me, "Words have power, little girl." I learn that lesson here in this village. And in order to end this sad period of a restrained existence, I have to play the role of everyone's "little girl." I don't share any of my secrets with them, but I fear that a romance with one of the village boys would feed their whisperings. For my own peace of mind, and that of our families, I refuse to entertain the thought.

Outings with the girls are much like a ritual. We hide from the villagers constantly spying on us. Several of us go to gather milk from the farm. Once the Madous are gone, we go to one farther away. We hurry on the way there so we can meet up with some boys seated on their scooters, who have come from the neighboring town. We talk. Not more than twenty minutes, beyond that it becomes suspicious. We trade idiocies, fill the silence with nothings, and one day, to avoid being unmasked, I mirror the other girls. I quickly kiss on the lips a handsome young man who's liked me for a long time, then add a "see you tomorrow." The walk home among girlfriends is gleeful. We talk, we laugh, and I conclude with, "No, definitely not, I don't like him." I rein myself in. I protect myself from the unhappiness curbing my every enthusiasm like a dead shadow. Then the prospect of a wasted life I had hoped to see crumble comes back. Return to my readings at the dinner table as if to better keep my feet on the ground. A struggle against a father who doesn't want to go easy on me. A dignified combat he cannot deny me.

I come downstairs and put a few endives to boil for your lunch, then I ask you in your language, "Maman, how did your father acquire his lands?" I want another story. After you, I'll run dry. Smiling, you say, "What I'm going to tell you is true." It's the story of the Sheik n'Tabla Sidi Ammar and his seven disciples. One especially harsh winter night, a brotherhood seeks in vain some hospitality while crossing an impoverished and austere region en route to a place of pilgrimage. But it's no use. Convinced they don't deserve such guests, the villagers shut themselves up in their homes and call on God. Through prayer, they ward off an inevitable misfortune of which they themselves will be the cause. The strengthening storm, pelting the supplicants with cold, moves the most destitute villager, Sidi Mohand, to pity. He brings the pilgrims into his humble home and has them sit next to the fire. They take off their burnoose cloaks and thank him piously. Then the poor man slaughters his only baby goat for them and hands it to his wife. Fatma Issounal quickly draws some milk and sets to her task in the stable. She cuts the meat and runs a string between the pieces, which she then places in a broth. She's barely dipped them into the liquid when a surprising and ill-fated thing occurs. All the scorching hot meat spurts out of the cauldron and spills onto the body of her only child. He drops dead. She screams. She screams with all her force. Her cries alert Sidi Mohand, who rushes over to say her behavior is disgraceful. "Stop crying, our guests will hear you," he tells his wife. Fatma Issounal, wracked with grief, shows him the child. Covered in burns and blood. The father, gripped by horror, says, "I will ask the sheik what we did to deserve such an ordeal. Cover him." Adding as he leaves, "It's a sign from God." The pilgrims, who were singing praises during this time, are unaware of the drama unfolding around them. They continue to say their prayers, eat their meal, and give thanks to their host until late into the evening. At dawn, Sidi Mohand takes the sheik aside. He tells him what took place even as his household was sheltering pious men. "In what way did I wrong God to merit such misfortune?" he asks. "In several months, you will have two sons, twins," responds the sheik. "You will name the first one Saïd. You will lean on him. The second one, Ali. Through him you will rise. After we leave, take your animals to graze near Djema n'Timulin. You will meet an old man there. A hermit. You will ask him to show you the place known as the Stone of Timulin n'Cherif. In this spot you will see two snakes coiled up against each other. One will turn its head toward the west, toward the sea, the other toward the east, toward the sun. At night, you will return to that spot. You will slide your hand between the two snakes and dig a hole. They will not wake. There, you will find your fortune. You will thank the old man and bury the rest of the gold in your house. You mustn't tell this story to anybody. Not even your wife. When your sons reach the age of fourteen, you will give each his share and make them leave for seven years. You will send Saïd to the French military academy and Ali to the best madrasah. When both of them return, you will be a rich man. You will leave for a stretch of land that they will split."

"Once Saïd becomes a caïd," you say, "he collects his parents from the village and settles with them in Tigzirt. The land that he shared with his brother stretched from Dellys to Azeffoun. Your grandfather, my father, is Saïd's son. He had eight girls and four boys. Three of those sons would become caïds in their turn. My father was the only one to refuse this calling. They governed all the towns in the region." I ask you to remind me about each member of this lineage. I hear beautiful names: Micha, Tétoum, Fta. Smiling, I tell you that it can't all be true. That the land was stolen, pillaged, or acquired by my ancestors via an unnatural alliance. "They didn't take property that belonged to someone else?" I ask you. "No," you respond. "It's all true." So I softly say, "That money might have belonged to another family, to rebels, to a dispossessed family that hid its Louis d'or coins for safekeeping."

"It was a Roman treasure, buried for centuries," you say. "And it's the Sheik n'Tabla Sidi Ammar who showed the way."

When you finish your lunch, you add, "The Romans erected a city facing the sea. It was swallowed up and no one came back to live in what became a swampy plain. The Kabyle people live far from the sea, protected, in the mountains. Your ancestors were the first to dwell in the Roman city. They built their homes up high, and with force and will they transformed it into an orchard."

As I left my mother, I wondered what empowered her to tell such a story. Her conviction about the way her family had acquired its lands emerged as if in defiance of the dispossession she herself had experienced. Ruling out all other possibilities, my mother was wholly immersed in the faraway time she was describing, in the telling of a miracle. The true story, so difficult to impose on her, might have flourished under more forgiving auspices. But when only adversity is left, I told myself, men draw on what they can. For that matter, I no longer believe what is written here and there about oral cultures. A vibrant energy ensures that these civilizations survive outside of texts and archives. Hence their cunning and resistance, especially when faced with violently irrational attitudes, as the speakers of these languages often are. A man from an oral culture carries his library within, and it's by transmitting it in the same way that he brings it to life. But my mother's certainty about the tale of hidden treasure conceals a crueler interpretation. The father had to hide the origins of his fortune. Either the money came from a theft or another family, who had hidden it, or the lands were acquired by means other than a straightforward monetary exchange. When the sheik makes it clear that the father will find protection with the son who is to join the French camp, one

can't help but think that the seed was already
planted. The French protection doesn't bring
any benefit. The sheik had said, "Ali in a madrasah to raise you up." And so the long path that
led my family to France was etched in its past.
You can find wealth and comfort by leaving your
family, but it means breaking with the values of
your kin.

What future can there be for a family narrative in a country that has erased all signs of it?
Expropriation, theft, servitude, and dispossession eat away at dignity, and from all this cruelty
emerges the deformed man. The degraded and
colonized man. Only a certain savoir-faire and
knowing duplicity can keep him alive. This rupture shattered everything literature has a duty
to express—the epic song of a people and all it
carries of their history and mission. A family saga
that my mother can perpetuate only through
tales and fables. Colonialism destroyed the heirs
to this legacy so that its memories would never

be passed on. And revolutionary, modern-day Algeria, to its greatest detriment, was unable to revive this—its own—past.

That afternoon, I looked at a photograph of my great-uncles and my grandfather. They are five, seated facing the camera. All very tall, handsome, and arrogant. Their faces are covered by beards, they're wearing thick, white turbans, beautiful kaftans gathered behind them, belts of beaded cloth that hold in ample white pants tucked into boots made of thick, black leather. They maintained their grandeur in what can be collectively called a farce. Holding on for dear life, the colonial power was forced to be complicit in this masquerade.

It's impossible to dominate with no one below you. What's there to do with an army but no enemy? What to do with settlers who were promised a better life under North African skies? The French authorities quenched the colonists' thirst for greatness through the figure of the beggar, the native. The man without rights, who would be made more indigent than the others. I don't question the suffering of the poor white man come to Algeria. Of the Alsatian fleeing the Germans. Of the impoverished Maltese, Spaniard, or Italian to whom were granted, just like the "Arab Jew," the stature of French citizen, even though, elsewhere in France, they were nothing. Even the advancement of a low-grade soldier, far removed from the officers' aristocracy, was accelerated. You can't reproach someone for being born there. But if everyone had had the same rights, another kind of uprising would have taken place in the French colony. Instead, social distinctions gave way to racial ones, and to a type of superiority more entrenched in the hearts of men.

In its beginnings, destitute captives from Europe carried out the colonial conquest of America. Both their jobs and statuses were lowly. Many of them revolted. And the colony grew more miserable still. It emptied Africa of its people. The prisoners and surviving slaves attempted to unite. But that alliance was broken. Only the white captive was granted emancipation. After several years of servitude, he would receive a few acres. Making him a pitiable, jealous landowner and the worse exploiter of the black man. Destitution was maintained through racial differences. If racism could have been overcome, an entirely different struggle would have taken place to the benefit of mankind. This ugly story is a vicious one. It drapes the perpetuator and victim alike in the narrow and binding garments available to them.

In my village the people I spend time with don't own books. None of them goes to the theater. No one listens to music. Cinema doesn't exist. Anything that could nurture a thought, a painting, art, history, or literature is foreign to the town's inhabitants. They are agricultural workers or factory employees. They don't pick their professions. If there is another model of what life can be, one more cultivated and ambitious, it has completely passed me by.

Many of the students at my junior high have violent and alcoholic fathers. For the most part their mothers wear gray-blue aprons, their faces aged by perms and their ankles swollen by work and pills. Except for the rare open-minded families—artisans mostly—everyone thinks it normal that I yield to their judgment. They can't imagine that I don't want to be just like them. I have to continually justify why I can't eat pork or drink alcohol, and the restrictions limiting my relationships with boys. It's by observing this narrow lifestyle and the absence of culture that I develop a taste for the outside world. I said I came from nowhere.

The problem is that the villagers believe their way of life is timeless. And I can't be a part of it unless I accept their customs. They eat pork, they drink wine, their women kiss men in public. That's the perimeter by which they evaluate their freedom. And it's enough. So I begin to eat pork and drink alcohol. But, because of my upbringing perhaps, I mask any romantic inclinations behind deeply rooted modesty.

My own curiosity grows in relation to their certitudes, and lack of interest in others. Nonetheless, I have to prove myself to this community.

I know that my readings have a strong influence on me when it comes to the injustice that has me telling my neighbors that I'm no different from them. It's true they aren't richer than I am. Their homes don't conceal any great inheritances. Formica, artificial oak, and acrylic armchairs are the materials that make up their daily lives. I don't live in a black ghetto in Memphis where everything would be off-limits, but in a white ghetto where all individuality is refused me. The word "God" is never pronounced in my presence, but I'm reproached for my parents' religion without being told why it's not as good as any other. In the villagers' minds, I'm Muslim, which for them equates to a kind of barbarism. They rank it below their own belief system in an act that valorizes and energizes their existence.

But God wasn't present at my birth. So I act outside of him, though not in ignorance of religious teachings. I have to justify to my family my refusal to believe. The villagers are spared this fight. Long ago they learned a prayer, which they imitate at funerals. For them, Jerusalem is not a place but the setting of the fable about baby Jesus, tucked into a corner of their brains. At school, they tell me to ignore everything that has to do with religion, but at home my mother punctuates her every sentence with a respectful

mention of God. I am so closed off to these invo-
cations that I educate myself about religion and
its justifications to show my parents that I am in-
formed and opinionated on the subject. I aspire
to another life. I want another one. A sentiment
I cannot share.

When my father is out, I go to his room and
face the sole full-length mirror in the house. I
sit down and talk to it. I speak to a presence. A
man I name Paul. I tell him everything. I talk. I
summon him over and over again. I ramble dis-
creetly for hours. "Paul, what if . . ." "Paul, what
if I lived with a French boy?" "Paul, what if . . ."
And it goes on. He answers me.

More than a mere secret, these forays into
madness terrify me.

I dream of neither a voyage nor a country,
but instead imagine myself under water probing
the ocean's depths. Carried away, though I don't
understand why yet, I view the silence of the sea
as a symbol of otherness. This unknown universe

is the only one, the final one that can still accommodate my desire to exist in a world without violence. I write to Captain Cousteau and ask to join his team. In his response, he explains that I have to work hard at school and later attend the Oceanographic Institute of Monaco. I cry when I read his letter, knowing that my father will spend nothing on me. My dream crumbles.

At the age of thirteen I need money. I introduce myself to a family with two children that has just moved to the village. The father holds a new kind of job. He is a senior computer engineer. I tell them that I am sixteen. My sister, who works in another house, has her employer confirm it. I clean on Wednesdays and occasionally Saturdays. I take care of the children as well. Sometimes I stay the evening. I discover their library. They're Catholic. I open books and catalogues. I see angels, clouds, crosses, Jesus, Mary. Painters. I go to town and visit the bookstore inside the post office where my brother made his purchases. A woman, whom everyone calls Colette, listens to me attentively. I make my first request. "Hello, I'm Hocine's sister. I want a book about paintings." She displays her collection of art books and talks to me. She shows me pictures and talks to me about art. I leave with Modigliani. Thirty years have gone by and the woman who provided my books is still there. I also use my earnings to buy my clothes and pay for my school lunches. When I can't respond to the follow-up letters sent by the school, I tell the principal that I don't have enough money. He's understanding, spares me the shame of being pulled from the line at lunchtime, as others are. This man, getting on in years, is bald, commanding, and strict. He terrorizes the students but welcomes me into his office with nothing but great kindness. Later I learn that he lived in Algeria. But I credit his indulgence to my excellent school results. I show up at my diploma ceremony brimming with confidence. The results are announced in the local press. The postwoman enters my home yelling at my mother, "Your daughter is first. First in Picardy." I am

number one across all the age groups. I already
knew this. The night before, I went to the prize
ceremony at the junior high in the presence of
the region's chairman, who is also the father
of my French teacher. I would have done anything for her. During the event, they ask me to
choose a book from among the three offered as
top prizes. They are long and beautiful. I comfort myself by picking *Underwater Exploration* and
pose for a photo with it. The picture of me surrounded by officials and teachers runs the next
day.

The best in Picardy? My mother is happy.
My father doesn't congratulate me, but I make
the best of it, convinced that for my whole life I
mustn't owe him anything. Mustn't owe anyone
anything. I've already stopped speaking to him.
My behavior is an affront to his sense of honor.
He reproaches me for going to school and the
havoc it wreaks within me. He wants to bring
me back in line. He forbids me the things that
I enjoy. Scarred by his past, he tells me, "Here,
you will be nothing. You are nothing." I seek out

my mother even more. I claim to need a bedroom with a desk, with my eye on a room on the
ground floor that will allow me to come and go
without their permission. I obtain the bedroom,
but I'm not fooling myself. No career path ap-
peals to me. Apart from telling stories to my
younger brothers, nothing suits me.

In junior high, my experience with education leaves me feeling extinguished. Around me,
no one is dreaming of a better future. There are
no scholars or artists in the village. No passion.
People are factory workers during the week and
farm laborers on the weekend. An interest in
their children might have paved a path to dia-
logue between our generations. But most of our
fathers are nowhere to be found apart from the
local bars. Once uninhibited by alcohol, they
allow themselves a lustful glance, telling me,
"Sweetheart, I'd love to jump in bed with you."
These men are happy to see me hanging around
outside, and satisfied that I find pleasure in their
company. Understanding that I am worth some-

thing, for a time I help them build some self-respect, degraded as they are to be men who count for little. They spend the winter outside, pouring the needed harvests into the ovens at the beet plant or braving the freezing cold to cut down poplars whose offshoots will be cultivated in the frigid, water-drenched soil. It's when their hands can make up for what they spend that these men, through their skills, regain their dignity. But beyond auto mechanics, home improvement, and the seasonable expertise of farming, these workers can't hold a conversation. In an effort to fight back against the ignorance enveloping them, they attach an obsessive importance to their own merits, namely the ability to take a blow. They are distrustful of my generation and turn up their noses at the awareness emerging within us and its reliance on foreign cultures. Like my father, they don't know what paternity can be. They go home exhausted, conscious of what has been made of them. Sitting at the table in silence, scrubbing off the dirt so they can take their wives properly, playing their masculine role for a moment in front of their kids, then sprawling on the couch with heavy weariness. Countless times, embarrassed, I hide with my friends in their bedrooms in order to shut out this unhappiness.

We live in a world without resources. It's decaying. Jobs are limited to the preparation and transportation of goods. The growing number of women who work reupholster chairs or make curlers. No revolution has affected them. We can't talk to them of politics or culture, and they don't know the name of a single philosopher or writer. Their daughters, whom they dress in acrylic sweaters and pleated miniskirts that excite the sons as much as the dads, dream about the singers of the era: Mike Brandt, Johnny Hallyday, Frédéric François. When some of us choose to cover up our bodies with layered skirts dyed in India, eyes lined in black powder, curled hair reeking of patchouli, our fathers start to hate us with a passion, questioning what possible role we can fill dressed like this. The violence dealt us—"the degenerate junkies"—is meant to drown out any response and weaken our desire to break free.

The young people in the village foresee a future much like that of their parents, who are completely satisfied with the comatose lives they lead. A little like the long duration of the Cold War that will eventually eclipse all the significance of the victory achieved by the Allies. Mainly the Americans who, envied for their flamboyance, are on occasion more disliked than us, "the Arabs."

What saves them is elsewhere. In the perpetuation of agricultural expertise and its benefits.

Unlike me, all the villagers know the taste of blueberries, gooseberries, blackcurrants, and wild mulberries. They know how to recognize with one glance the slightest sign of vegetative plants. Starting in March, the countryside comes to life with activity that occupies many of the children. Everyone has to do his or her part of the hard work, the planting, weeding, watering, and maintenance, which they learn by listening and observing. I owe the diligence I apply to being a good gardener to my sister, whom I avoid like the plague. On days with no school, I earn money to give to my family. I refuse to be judged poorly for working. I learn a lot about gardens. First from curiosity and then from inclination. My mother leaves the upkeep of the house to my sister (who spends most of her time there) and is solely concerned with logistics, our happiness, and her vegetable garden.

She works there from morning to night and through her exertions reawakens something inside herself. She greets each plant and flower at length, and talks to the hens and the few caged rabbits. When they become too numerous, she lets them out. Cheep, cheep, and off they go toward the fields.

"Maman, the hunters will kill them."

"No."

The day she decides to free all the caged animals is etched in my memory. My brother

Ammar had dropped off his friend's aviary for the summer. Twenty-four birds. Two lovebird couples and some parakeets. Cheep, cheep, cheep, and up and away.

"Maman, they're going to die. They can't live in the wild."

"No."

As a child, my mother used to have a pet rabbit. She can't imagine that people eat rabbits in France. She also had a donkey, a horse, and a goat. She asks my father for the latter. Everything is coming alive for her. The Oise region, despite the climate, is enough for her to relive the joys and tastes of her childhood. She is so insistent about getting her goat that my father finally brings home a lamb. But he made an unfortunate assumption. Scooby-Doo will not be eaten. The lamb accompanies my mother as she works and sometimes follows us along the path to school. At night, he knocks at the front door with his small hoof. We open it and he enters the living room, settles down in his chosen spot, on a sheepskin, and watches the evening news with us. We are moved by his kindness and intelligence. He is gentle, clean, and affectionate. One day, he follows me to the farm across the street, hesitates on the sidewalk, crosses too late, a car hits him. A loud noise, I backtrack, Scooby-Doo is dead. I blame myself, I cry. The driver tells me, "It's okay, you can make roasted lamb out of it." The man leaves me crying on the asphalt, holding Scooby-Doo's bleeding head. We give him a dignified burial under the big tree in the garden. We throw flowers on him. Now that he's dead, we want another one. My brother brings us a frail and abandoned poodle. A sad little face like you rarely see. We name him Izmir and I can say that, for fear that he'll stray too far, the dog spends as much time in the garden as we do.

The garden is composed of four large plots. The main one is intended for potatoes, the second for onions and garlic, the third for staked crops and thin green beans, peas, and fava beans. We add peppers, chickpeas, and herbs. Coriander, cumin, and mint. The last plot is dedicated to carrots, turnips, artichokes, zucchinis, and other gourds. The provisions we accumulate for the year are enough to feed us. We unearth the potatoes, which we spread out in a storeroom. We let the onions dry for a few days, then tie them in braids to be hung up. When it's time for the canning, together we peel the tomatoes dunked in hot water to make coulis. The children shell the peas and, if they're dexterous, string the green beans. The gardening season always ends with preserves, which we store in a laundry room dedicated to that purpose. Then we let winter roll by. Once the cold is gone, we dig into the hard earth with a spade. Everyone has a go at it. They have to.

The work in the village is shared and anyone can be called upon to lend a hand. The difficulty is such that we pay someone to help us. The father of a friend. He's the first villager to regularly spend time with us. A good, simple man who likes wine and talking to people. He comes often and then every day. His curiosity about us

is not entirely innocent. It feeds his bistro con-
versations. So we have to make an ally of him.
When he's around us, he eats and laughs constantly. He puts his bottle of wine in a shrub to
stay cold as he works and takes gulps while my
mother's back is turned.

"Take the shovel, little girl, and watch what
I'm doing."

He explains how to prepare the soil. Turn it
over and remove the roots. I concentrate. I dig.
I do it again, I keep going. He teaches me how
to use gardening twine, what distance to put between the seeds, how to hoe furrows on a gentle
slope, the way to set up stakes, the maturity of a
vegetable and the care it needs, how to remove
roots with thick leaves, how to snip the tops off
carrots and turnips, the proper development of
a pumpkin, how to trim trees and rosebushes,
how to graft a cherry tree, and, on top of everything else, he takes me to visit other vegetable
patches. I memorize the different kinds of crops,
I buy books, I learn the science of gardening,
botany, and the classification of species. An ap-

preciation for the work we're doing will connect me to this land and its people. Over time the fruit trees and decorative plants will multiply. Today grass lawns have overrun the gardens. We aren't any richer, but the price of food is much lower than the cost of the effort and seedlings invested. The transmission and preservation of this type of knowledge has completely stopped. I saw it all disappear over a few short years. I can't resign myself to it. Today, I share my passion like a Holy Grail with those of my friends in Paris who, like me, saw this lifestyle disappear.

Every year, during the third weekend in August, a village festival with merry-go-rounds and music is held behind our house. A lantern procession launches the festivities on Friday night. Led by the city council and the school principal, the parade gathers together all the students in town. It passes in front of each home and parents come to the door to wave as their children go by. The first time, I'm not allowed to attend the festival. I watch the procession from behind the window shutters, which remain closed. The following year I convince my mother to take my sister and me. She waits until my father, who has a separate bedroom, falls asleep. It's dark. She spreads quilts on our beds, puts on European clothes, crosses the field that separates our house from the gazebo, and enters the large ballroom tent with us.

The villagers greet her in shock. She remains seated, smiling, and encourages us to have fun. I introduce her to my schoolmates. Her awkward "hello" moves me. Unlike my father, she doesn't understand the song lyrics and therefore, seeing our good mood, can't imagine that they evoke any kind of vice. Throughout the night I do my best to cling to my new girlfriends and ignore the boys. If they approach, it will cost me as much as it will them. And they know it. The joyful, talkative gardener has taken care to explain our lifestyle in all its severity. "You know, their father never laughs." And a few words about us, his poor daughters.

My mother wants to see us happy. We return home without making any noise.

Village festivals punctuate the summer. They take place in other towns as well, situated a handful of miles away. Sometimes we hear fireworks and echoes of dancing. They all last three days and have the same program. Lantern procession on Friday night, opening of the merrygo-rounds when the children arrive, then a ball held under a large gazebo with a band. Often the same one, led by a singer with bleached hair

who imitates French pop stars. He's always accompanied by a new conquest with dyed hair,
heavy makeup, and tight clothes. The band
singers are local legends, shadowed by young
women dreaming of a life made better by the
mere effect of their artificial hair color. They approach the stage as rivals, in search of glory. On
Saturday, the bumper cars are taken by storm,
serving as preludes to the encounters that take
place at night behind the gazebo. Two girls drive
a car and chase two guys. Then the guys chase
the girls. After three rounds, they meet up at the
refreshment stand, talk for a few minutes, and
everyone goes home to get decked out for that
evening's conquest. Sunday is for families and
the raffle. People visit the different shooting galleries to win a teddy bear or a baseball hat. Parents arrive at the ball with their children, showing off their sons- and daughters-in-law. The
majorettes' parade is in the afternoon. Drums
and batons and all the girls jealously eyeing the
prettiest one there. My father hates this kind of

exhibition. Then comes the last day to dance. Monday afternoon, reserved for the old folks. A shift in register. Waltz or mambo. We attend anyway, to keep it going, telling ourselves the fun will be in mocking them. But we end up imitating them. We're horrible, but they tolerate us.

In my last year of junior high, fate has it that I meet two high school girls. They have a home filled with books and an Italian father. I'm struck by the blondness of his hair. I go to their house by bus or on foot. Their father fascinates me. He talks politics to me. I learn that he's an immigrant from northern Italy, that he has Austrian roots, that he's a worker at the chemical plant. He and his wife act happy when they're around their family, they love their daughters, and lunchtime is the occasion for debates that teach me about the history of struggle. I borrow their books, soothed by their political engagement. I read in their garden and begin a relationship with my new friends that will eventually turn my life upside down. We put up fliers and travel across the entire region. One night in Paris I listen to some Trotskyist leaders. I leave my bedroom very early in the morning and get into a car waiting for me outside. We leave to sell newspapers at the factory exit. It's the change-over from the night crew and a man tells me nicely that it's time to go to sleep. Two of us hold a red scarf, in which coins have been tossed, while shouting, "Demand the *Workers' Struggle*."

"Honey, it's time for bed."

"Demand the *Workers' Struggle*."

A person comes to this in an odd way. You don't understand everything. You're given a book. You read it, you're shaken. You want another one. Once again, you're rattled. One more. That's how you get started. John Reed, Jack London, Erich Maria Remarque, Joseph Conrad. More books. You earn several francs. Books. Every week, I go to a meeting and talk to an activist. I talk about my readings, the text and the subject. The session always takes place in a café and sometimes lasts a long time. Someone suggests another book, I buy it, I read it. They give me booklets, manuals, and manifestos. Marx, Engels, Trotsky. It sinks in all the same. And one beautiful day I tell a comrade my pseudonym, Galia, which I hope masks the partial anagram of Algiers. Galia, and I see myself caught within a universal mythology even as I cling to Algeria. And nowhere to go.

"Maman, tell me why we don't go back?"

"Your father can't."

"And without him, we can't?"

"They won't want us."

"Well, nobody wants us. What do we do? Stay?"

No answer. And not a North African friend in sight. I could have asked him or her if they intended on returning. They no doubt would have told me, "Yes." Would I have believed it at the time?

I discuss politics more and more frequently. I abandon my family as required, but without stealing from them like the others ask. I work nonstop, I babysit, I clean houses, I contribute my share to the struggle, but I don't forget my English melodies and my girlhood hopes.

One summer, there is a three-day music festival under the stars on the Mount. A friend and I decide to spend the night there, thrilled to stay up late out in the open, amid the sounds of conversation and gunshots. Bang, bang, a clay pigeon shoot. An imaginary hunt at the edge of a wood that attracts all those thirsting for life. But to hell with the guns if we can have fun. Of my childhood memories, this is the most beautiful moment. We dance for three nights on a makeshift floorboard, with a bird's-eye view of the horizon and surrounded by the pleasant laughter of people gathered together, pacified for the occasion like a calm sea. We talk, we laugh, we eat. We climb down to quickly wash up and then climb back. In one stroke, the village has opened to everyone and a crowd of curious people is walking between hill and road. It's blissful. Far from the shots, at the wood's entrance, four boys seated around a fire silently listen to one of their own sing. Plucking the strings of a guitar, he plays a ballad that I've hummed a thousand times. Rifle shots mingle with the friendly words of teens openly living out their pacifist utopia. The boys smoke, drink beers, and speak to us with a softness we have rarely heard. We start to sing, in awkward English, the fullness of the moment. Occasionally collecting, one after the other, firewood that will warm us until morning. They come from nearby, they're good and good-looking. The one singing has an unusual face, his left eye almost shut. He's tall and moves his body like a supple cord, and exudes an admirable concern for others. I listen and watch him. I like him. The festival lasts three days. We don't sleep at night. In the morning we drink coffee and then when the sun rises we doze off in the grass.

"Where do you live?"

"Come on, I'll show you."

We walk to the peak of the Mount and I point out the home from which I've fled.

"Do you see it? You see the big tree over there. It's at the edge of my garden. It's a Canadian pine. That's my house."

He tells me his name. His dad is a carpenter. I've heard of his parents' business. We walk along the ridge and I learn that he's a student.

I tell him, "I'm supposed to go to Clermont high school, as a boarder. But there's no transportation to get there."

"I spend the week in Amiens. I can drop you off on Mondays and pick you up on Fridays on my way back."

"My father will refuse to pay."

And we keep walking. We rejoin our friends.

He wants to change and asks me to accompany him. We climb down the Mount, we run, we hold hands, and I get into his car. A few miles away, we stop in front of a porch. I'm embarrassed, we enter the house.

"Mom, I'd like you to meet a friend."

And he goes upstairs to shower. I stay with his mother.

"What's your name?"

I'm filled with emotion. I feel like I'm saying my name for the first time.

"Welcome to our home. Do you want coffee?"

I'm taken aback. I'm scared. I fall in love.

I have coffee with her.

"Is my son good to you?"

I'm confused. Such kindness. I don't have the right. And already I'm getting carried away. I love him, I love his mother.

"Yes, very."

"He takes after his father. While we wait, come outside and hang the laundry with me."

We pin up the clothes in the garden. Then she shows me some very high plants.

"My son teases me," she says. "I know they're not aromatic plants. Look, they're taller than I am."

He joins us laughing.

"If I tell you what they are, you'll tear them out, so I won't say anything. Come on, let's go."

He kisses his mother, who kisses me in turn.

I'm silent in the car. I'm building a house of cards. I see myself living with him and his parents. We find our friends again, the party

continues. My boyfriend is cheerful and everyone is talking about us. The last dance begins,
we move together, waving about wildly, holding each other close, as if we've already become
a group united through pleasure. Others join
us and we transform into a friendly circle that
forces the band to accept our requests for livelier
and more popular songs, effortlessly covering
beloved hits by singers like Claude François and
Dalida, which we sing as we jump and do a few
faster moves so they'll play a good song by Elvis
or "Sex Machine." We hope to push back the
hunters, leaving us to reign alone on the dance
floor, and make the band justify its presence with
a performance worthy of whoever of our group
is on stage playing the rock star. Already the entire place belongs to us, excluding those watching from a victory that isn't hurting anyone but
which they settle with small, bitter words, ac-
cusing us of drinking more than just beer. But
I'm not doing anything after all but finally experiencing a freedom long hoped for. We continue until we're sweaty, the night air cools us

off, and then my boyfriend grabs the guitar, succumbs to the pleasure of playing. Leaving the singer on the sideline, he uses his voice as if it were enchanted, shutting up all those who think we're not worth anything, but a country boy who sings in a foreign language and who furthermore is the boss's son can't be silenced, so we all get closer and listen to him pronounce the beautiful words of love of those over there in the United States who make us cherish freedom for what it has that is unique and rare and that we're experiencing at this moment as if it's come true. In chorus our voices tell the hunters:

> Guess what, your kids are nothing like you
> cowards hiding in a grave that's gonna be the end
>   for us all
> your glorious generation is sucking us dry
> your generation is burying us
> you glean satisfaction from little but your camping
>   trips
> you mock intelligence when you have none
> you prefer the dog to the starving man
> you shoot at birds as we protest murder

you pick at the good fat still eroding the bone
you beg our bodies which refuse your rapes

—and like that, my boyfriend stuns them. Eyes
closed, he invites these men who kill animals out
of habit to stop once and for all.

The sun comes up. And the party will last all
summer.

Back from the Mount, my father chases me
away. "Slut." I take my things and move into a
friend's house. Her parents leave for a few days.
Happiness on the horizon.

Here we are again, there's six of us. We com-
bine our savings, we go shopping as if for a
family. I stop at my house and grab a couple
of records. I tell my mother, "I promise you, I
won't do anything wrong. I want to live. Finally
experience a vacation. Two weeks and then I'll
be back." She begs me not to take any risks.

My politically minded friends tell me I'm behaving badly. I respond that I just want this moment and then I'll stop. Then I'll be available

and all theirs. I leave them. I wasn't lying. I'm
sure of it. But I'm chastised regularly. "You're
lost." "You're in way over your head." I respond,
"I promise, I'm one of you." But I want the
things I have yet to experience.

I'm not even sixteen. The summer is wonderful. The six of us take a car to go on a pic-
nic. We venture beyond our boundaries. We
visit new places. We feel connected and united.
Others join us. Our drives are packed. At night
we go back to a house. A parent's or friend's.
We learn how to make a few basic dishes with
joyful clumsiness. We kick balls in the street,
we steal flowers from gardens, we give them to
one another for a special occasion, happy holiday. And we laugh until the next one. We dance
as we sing blues songs, imitating some of black
music's greatest figures. We experiment with
sounds, with instruments. For me it's the accor-
dion, I play like an Yvette Horner overcome by
rhythm. We improvise farcical skits about the
lives that we loathe. We don't sleep, we barely
eat, we laugh, we run away to the sea, we eat

mussels, and we return at night. We throw ourselves into the nocturnal waters of a neighboring pond, enter the orchards, crunch on fruits hidden in the grass. We scare one another in the dark forest, the trees picking up the echo of our voices, lighters in hand, bolting at the slightest noise, waiting for dawn, leaping roebucks, feeding ourselves with strawberries as tiny as teeth, rolling our bodies in beech leaves, smelling nature as if with a snout, imitating the wildlife we rarely see, despite our ever patient and silent efforts. We come home still starving. We make a meal out of sausages and chips, which my friends wash down with beer. I can't stand the taste. But I'm funny and good at pranks so it's like I already have some alcohol in reserve. This is the life we were waiting for. Loving as if by enchantment these boys who are nothing but gentle. An unmarred harmony that we hope will last forever. But how? Love scares me. It's agonizing. Unfathomable. So I get rid of it through games and evasion.

* * *

"I promise, Maman, I won't do anything wrong."

My face is pure radium. Dazzling smile, boundless generosity and a full heart. But what can I do? What can I do besides cry? I deny myself, as aware of the seductiveness of the taboo surrounding me as of the strength it gives me. In total control, I prolong my life by distancing anything that could, in my father's mind, mean my negation. No alcohol, no drugs, no boys. I think I'll make it out like this. Through will alone. I am not a bitch or a whore. I love my family. My brothers and even more so the three youngest, who I want to protect. I want to love them without fear. They shouldn't be responsible for my virginity. In France, I can't reconcile this timeless law with anything. Not that you can anywhere else. It hangs above my head like a sword. Each time my boyfriend takes my hand, it burrows painfully into my skull. I see it constantly. It's in my dreams. The sword burrows in, and behind it is my mother. Silent and resigned. So I break away from my darling, who wants nothing but good for me. He thinks that restraint and time will ease the moment.

The summer ends.

What can I do? I can't head off to high school. In two weeks I will be sixteen. My mother has no money. I can't be a boarder. My father refuses. I knock on every door. I want to go to school. The party is over. I beg my father. I beg him to let me study. My mother is powerless. She's always by my side. But this is beyond her, she can't do anything.

One night I write her a letter, to thank her. I slip it under my bed. Dear Maman. I want to sleep for a long time. I love you. And under the sheets, I swallow.

That night, she approached in the dark. Her instinct, her love pushed her to enter my bedroom.

She told me, "First I touched you. Then I spoke to you and then I shook you. I shook you very hard." Then she screamed.

They say her shouts woke up everyone in the village.

Epilogue . . .

I thought I would find you alone on your couch, but I see you stretched out, holding a small body in your arms. Your newest grandson, to whom you're murmuring words in your language. I hear you call him, "Cébien. Cébien." I correct you, "He's called Esteban, Maman. Esteban. It's a Spanish name. Spanish, like his mother."

You look at me and, turning back to him once more, your son's child, you repeat, "Cébien, Cébien."

"Esteban. Es-te-ban, Maman."

"Cébien," you keep saying.

I leave you for a moment. You aren't going to let this little one go so soon after his father has brought him to you. He recognizes those whispers you slip into his son's ear. That gift you have is what kept him going too. Just like me.

I have faith.

ZAHIA RAHMANI is a French author and art historian whose works include three novels: *Moze, "Muslim": A Novel,* and *France, Story of a Childhood.* Born in Algeria, Rahmani resides in Paris and the Oise region of France and directs the Art and Globalization research program at France's National Institute for Art History.

LARA VERGNAUD is an editor and translator. Her translations from the French include works by Ahmed Bouanani, Mohand Fellag, Joy Sorman, Marie-Monique Robin, and Scholastique Mukasonga. She lives in Washington, D.C.